Tales of Castle Vasile

Written by Josh Cuny

Illustrations by Corrine Smith

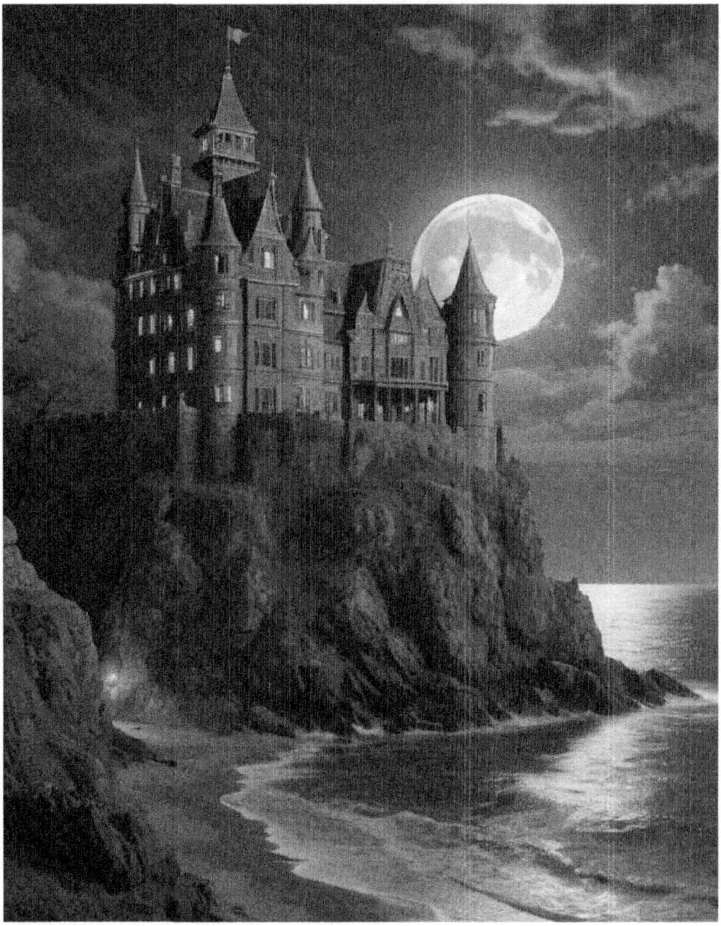

Table of Contents

Tale 1: Initiation of Blood	5
Chapter 1	5
Chapter 2	17
Chapter 3	20
Tale 2: Armand and Elena	28
Chapter 1	28
Chapter 2	36
Chapter 3	45
Chapter 4	49
Tale 3: The Client and the Case	59
Chapter 1	59
Chapter 2	65
Chapter 3	70
Tale 4: The Vasile Order	77
Chapter 1	77
Chapter 2	100
Chapter 3	109
Tale 5: New Year's Eve	118
Chapter 1	118
Chapter 2	128
Chapter 3	135

Tale 6: The Vampire and The Serpent   146

       Chapter 1   146

       Chapter 2   149

       Chapter 3   165

Tale 7: The Master and the Student   171

       Chapter 1   171

       Chapter 2   183

TALE 1: INITIATION OF BLOOD

CHAPTER 1

On a cool and crisp autumn evening in late eighteenth-century Scotland, a horse drawn carriage is traveling towards the town of Kirkcaldy. Mist begins to fill the air and fog gradually appears. The aroma of cool autumn rain fills the carriage and is felt by the passenger, a young and beautiful Scottish lass by the name of Margaret McGregor, who is taking a journey on the carriage from Dundee onto Edinburgh to meet with her fiancé, but the driver believes it is best to stop for the night in Kirkcaldy due to the late time and for possible severe weather.

The auburn-haired, blue-eyed beauty observes outside the carriage and notices the fog, and then is startled to hear the sound of a rabid wolf howling which concerns

Margaret and questions whether there should be wolves in this part of Scotland.

Listening to the frightening howl of the wolf, feeling penetrating drops of rain and suddenly hears a crackle of thunder, the driver is anxious to arrive in the city and find an inn to stay for the night. The driver cracks the whip on the two burley horses pulling the carriage as the horses gallop faster.

A pesky bat flies past the driver's head. "Get away from me you bloody, flying rodent", yells out the driver. A disturbing feeling consumes the horses as the driver begins to panic as the cry of the wolf gets closer and the cold rain falls with a little more force.

Inside the carriage, Margaret hears an awful growl coming from the top of the carriage as well as a shriek of pain from the driver. Abruptly, the carriage takes off, going faster and faster. Margaret screams as she cries out, "Help, somebody help! Please, God help!". But nobody, not even God hears her plea for help. The horses break free from the carriage which then collapses on its side.

Margaret is still conscious and attempts to free herself by opening the adjacent door which is now facing upwards. Successfully opening the door, the disturbed young woman frantically climbs out of the carriage carrying her handbag. She lands on the ground and looks around for her luggage which were mounted on top of the carriage. There is no sign of her luggage anywhere. Margaret begins to panic because all of her belongings, including her clothes and jewelry were contained in the duel travel cases.

Margaret looks around to locate the driver. A few meters away, she spots a body lying on the ground and runs hastily towards the body of the driver who is laying face first in a muddy puddle of water.

Margaret is apprehensive as she turns the body towards her, then jumps back in fear and screams at the top of her lungs. She is shocked and horrified by the site of the driver's body, whose throat has been shredded apart and head is nearly decapitated.

In desperation, Margaret takes off her set of heels and runs in terror from the site of the carnage. She is full of dread that maybe that wolf or whatever beast murdered the driver could still be out there. Could this beast be stalking her at this moment?

Margaret feels in between her wet toes the gooey sensation of filth and sludge. She stops for a moment to catch her breath and looks all around and carefully listens but does not hear howls anymore.

Margaret looks straight ahead into the dark night and the fog which is getting denser. But there is hope as she views a light from afar. Margaret thinks that perhaps it is a house and hopefully by the grace of God there is someone home who can help and hurries towards the dazzling light.

The falling coarse rain begins to fall on Margaret's head as she runs faster and faster. She comes to a bridge which leads to what appears to be a castle and notices several lit candles in the windows of the castle. An intense light emanating from the lantern at the front entrance.

The weary and frightened young woman runs across the bridge and notices the castle and the grounds are surrounded by the ocean which now has a layer of fog covering the water.

Finally, Margaret makes it to the front door and knocks loudly on the door hoping someone is home.

She hears faint footsteps from the other side of the door which begins to slowly creaks open and at once, a tall, slender, old Scotsman is seen by Margaret, looking down on her. The old man asks," Good evening my lass, how may I help you?"

Margaret responds frantically," I really need your help, kind sir. I was just in an awful carriage accident. The driver is dead, and I have lost my belongings except for what I have in this small handbag. Can you help me? Are you the lord of this castle."

The old man replies with assurance," I am but a servant of Castle Vasile, but I am sure that Count and Countess Vasile will be more than willing to help. Why don't you come on in out of the rain?

Margaret enters the castle and says," Thank you so much kind sir." Margaret walks into the front foyer of the castle which is somewhat dreary and dark. But the smell of old leather and lit candles permeate the foyer The old man replies," My name is Argyle,"

Margaret eagerly replies," It is nice to meet you Argyle, my name is Margaret, Margaret McGregor."

Argyle says," Well, Miss Margaret why don't you follow me into the lounge. You can rest on the sofa, which is quite comfortable. Also, I just built a fire which will help warm you up. In the meantime, I will alert the Count and Countess to your presence and your plight."

Sitting down on the sofa in the lounge area, Margaret detects the scent of burning oak from the fireplace. The lounge is fairly shadowy with just the light of the fireplace and a lantern at the opposite end of the room. She looks around and marvels at the elegance of the room and the size of the rather large fireplace, which is so large, Margaret could almost walk right into it without bending down. Above the fireplace there is a large painting of a man and woman dressed formally.

Margaret points at the painting and asks," Is that the Count and Countess of the Castle Vasile?" Argyle answers," Why yes. They had that made sometime a year ago."

Before Argyle can take his leave, a boisterous voice is heard from the hallway, a young Scotsman's voice," Argyle, I didn't know we had company", says the Scotsman.

Argyle responds," Oh, Master Ryan, this young lass was involved in a terrible accident down the road from here. I was about to locate the Count and Countess."

Ryan says." They are both in the study. I am sure they will want to meet Miss…?" Margaret replies," Margaret McGregor."

Ryan walks towards Margaret and gentle grabs her hand and kisses Margaret's hand delicately and says," I am Ryan McAllen, the son of Count and Countess Vasile and it is a pleasure to meet you. I hope you are alright'.

Argyle states," I will get your parents, Master Ryan".

As Argyle leaves the lounge, Margaret says to Ryan," I am feeling better now, just a little scared. The driver was attacked by some kind of beast, a wolf, I think. The driver's throat was ripped apart. It was so awful and gruesome".

Margaret begins to tremble in fear when Ryan places his hand on her shoulder and says," You are safe now here at our home." Ryan walks over the bar stand which sits in front of a large liquor cabinet and asks," Can I interest you in a drink perhaps some cognac."

Margaret answers meekly," Yes, please but just a small glass will do." Ryan pours a drink for both Margaret and himself and walks over to Margaret and hands her the drink.

Taking a sip of the cognac, Margaret looks at Ryan and admires his dark red hair and asks," Forgive me for asking. Your surname is McAllen, yet your parents' name is Vasile?"

Ryan answers," Well, I was orphaned when I was twelve and Count and Countess took me in and gave me a home. So, they are my parents in every way that matters the most."

A deep Romanian voice is heard, "So Argyle, this is the lovely young Lady you spoke of", says Count Vasile as both Count and Countess Vasile make their entrance into the lounge with Argyle following loyally behind.

Count Vasile, who is tall and muscular with dark hair and his wife Countess Vasile, who has long dark hair and an hourglass figure. Both, however, have pail skin but Margaret is still enamored by how handsome Count Vasile is and how beautiful Countess Vasile is. Margaret thinks to herself neither one looks all that much older than Ryan.

Count Vasile says to Margaret, "I am Count Bogdan Vasile, and this is my wife Countess Mariana Vasile".

Margaret replies graciously," It is my pleasure and thank you for allowing me into your fine castle."

Countess Vasile says," It is our pleasure to help those in need. Just like Ryan, our son". Count Vasile says with concern," We heard about the awful accident and the death of your driver. How tragic."

Countess Vasile then asks," Are you hungry my dear?" Margaret replies" I am a bit hungry, my Countess." Countess Vasile remarks," Bogdan, she has such fine manners".

A loud crackle of thunder is heard shaking the castle and a flash of vivid lightning is seen through the windows and Margaret jumps from her seat. Ryan laughs and says" A bit jumpy, are we? Scared of thunder?"

Margaret replies" After the night I have had, a harmless fly might scare me."

Countess Vasile looks towards Argyle and asks," Argyle, is there any dinner left?

Argyle answers, "There is some lamb stew that Gertrude cooked from earlier."

Count Vasile tells Argyle," Go to the kitchen and have Getrude heat up some stew for our guest." Argyle answers," Yes my Count," Argyle makes his way to the kitchen.

Ryan adds," Gertrude is our cook and a fine cook at that, you will love her lamb stew." Margaret says with a smile," Lamb stew is one of my favorites."

Countess Vasile asks," Miss Margaret did you have any luggage with you?" Margret replies," I did but it was lost in the accident. All I have is the handbag."

Count Vasile looks towards Ryan and says," Once this storm has passed, go outside and see if you can locate Miss Margert's belongings." Ryan replies," Yes sir. Shall I get the guestroom ready for her?"

Countess Vasile answers," Yes and make it the main guestroom. We want nothing but the best for Miss Margaret McGregor."

Margaret replies," You are too kind my Countess and my Count and you as well Master Ryan. Please allow me to offer you some money for your trouble."

Count Vasile answers," We wouldn't think of it besides we enjoy having guests. Now let my wife and I escort you to the dining room.

Margaret is sitting at the lengthy dining table in the elegant dining room. There are five chairs on one side and five on the other with one chair at each end. The room is fairly light with candles all around the room on several mantles and three on the dining table. Margaret is sitting in the middle while Count Vasile sits on one end and Countess Vasile sits on the other end.

Gertrude, an older abrasive looking woman of German ancestry emerges from the kitchen with a large bowl of lamb stew and places it in front of Margaret and asks, "Would you like some more tea?"

Margaret replies," That would be nice. Thank you." Gertrude walks back to the kitchen as

Margaret takes a sip of her stew and asks Count and Countess Vasile, "This is delicious. Are you two not having any?" As she looks over to Countess Vasile and then to Count Vasile.

Countess Vasile answers," Oh, we have already had dinner." Count Vasile asks," So where were you travelling to, my dear?"

Margaret answers as Gertrude enters with some more tea and gently sets the cup by Margaret, "I was on my way to Edinburgh to meet with my fiancé, Bruce Andrews. I was going to stop at Kirkcaldy for the evening, but my driver and carriage was attacked by a wolf, I believe."

Count Vasile responds," Yes, we heard the tragic news. So, what kind of work does your fiancé do?"

Margaret replies," He works as a blacksmith with his father. We hope to marry next spring."

Count Vasile responds," Blacksmith, such a noble profession. I'm sure he will make a loving husband."

Countess Vasile says," And you, a loving wife. In the meantime, you are our honored guest. Tomorrow morning, we will see to it, that you make your way to Edinburgh."

Feeling relief Margaret appreciates the hospitality from the Vasile's and says," Thank you for your generosity." She then asks," May I ask where you are from. Your accents sound eastern European?"

Count Vasile answers, "Romania or Transylvania to be more specific, we came to Scotland many years ago to escape famine."

" Yes, we found this deserted castle, purchased it and, decided to make it our new home", adds Countess Vasile.

Gertrude and Argyle emerge from the kitchen and into the dining room. Argyle is carrying a large piece of luggage. Margaret sees the luggage and says with excitement, "Oh my, That's my luggage. Did Master Ryan find it?"

Argyle answers, "Yes, indeed. He located it not far from the carriage." "I need to offer him my gratitude", says Margaret.

Countess Vasile announces," After the kitchen is clean, Argyle, please take Miss McGregor's luggage to her room and Gertrude, please draw her a bath. I am certain she could use one after the night she has had."

Argyle and Gertrude nod and walk back into the kitchen. Margaret replies, appreciatively," Oh thank you all for your kindness and a bath would be nice."

Countess Vasile then stairs into Margaret's bright blue eyes. Margaret for the moment feels euphoric like there are no cares for the world. Then regains consciousness as Countess Vasile says, "Why don't you have some biscuits for desert. Then I will show you to your room."

*****

Argyle is standing in the kitchen. He is leaning on an old wooden table used for cutting and butchering. A homemade flytrap is laying on the table with several flies stuck to it. Argyle stairs at the flies with an intent look. He then grabs a fly from the trap and puts the fly in his mouth and begins crunching on the insect.

Gertrude, who has just finished preparing a bath for Margaret, enters the kitchen and walks straight to the flytrap, grabs a couple flies, and begins eating them.

Ryan enters the kitchen and says," Well if it isn't my two favorite ghouls." Argyle responds, "We are the only two ghouls you know." Ryan replies," Just as true. Looks like our Count and Countess will be having desert tonight."

A voice is heard from outside the kitchen," That is one way to put it.", says Count Vasile as he and Countess Vasile enter the kitchen.

Ryan asks," So, it would appear, that Miss Margaret meets your standards for initiation."

Countess Vasile responds," Yes much better than the last two individuals you brought into this castle. I can't believe they actually tried to steal from us."

Ryan says," Yes, my apologies. Life is without its lessons. I don't suppose I could start the initiation process. I am still hungry."

Count Vasile responds," I would think that carriage driver would have satisfied your hunger. Anyhow, you are not ready to start an initiation process."

Ryan, looking somewhat disappointed but not surprised as this was the reaction he had expected, responds, "She is a lovely little lass. So beautiful and full of spirit."

Countess Vasile says," It will be nice to have an addition to our family. But if you are still hungry there are some leftovers in the dungeon."

CHAPTER 2

Margaret is looking around the guest room and is impressed with the furnishings. The bed, which is quite sizable, is comfortable to the touch.

Margaret thinks to herself that she will get a good night's rest on this rainy and foggy evening.

There is a full body mirror in the corner of the room next to a vanity table with a smaller desk mirror. Margaret admires some of the paintings that decorate the walls of the room. There are paintings of werewolves and bats feeding on other animals. Normally, Margaret would be horrified by such images but for some strange reason, that even she cannot explain, finds a certain disturbing beauty in the paintings.

There is a glass double door that leads to an outdoor terrace. Margaret opens the doors and walks out onto the terrace, which overlooks the Atlantic Ocean. The storm has ceased but a light rain continues. The young, stranded lass can still feel and breath the heavy mist in the air. She is in awe of the fog that covers the surface of the ocean and now surrounds the castle.

Thinking to herself to herself, how grand it would be if she could live here forever. But finally, she has a commitment to her young and handsome fiancé, Bruce.

Margaret walks back inside the room towards the bathtub that sits in the middle of the room, and she begins to get undressed.

Outside the double glass doors, a bat flies outside around the terrace and views the Vasile's guest from outside. Stepping into the cozy tub Margaret begins bathing.

Meanwhile, outside on the terrace a heavy mist surrounds the bat, which transforms into a human form. That form being Count Bogdan Vasile, who admires the nude figure of the young Scottish Woman.

*****

In the dungeon of the castle which lies beneath, Ryan is carrying a torch as it is extremely dark in the dungeon. He walks up to a door which is locked. Ryan takes a key from his pocket and unlocks the door and enters a damp and dingy room with stone walls making up the perimeter of the room. A musty and damp stench fills the room as does the smell of rotten and decaying flesh.

A man and a woman are chained to one of the walls. They both are naked, grey skinned with several lesions covering their entire bodies. They look to be at least eighty years of age, but they are really in their early twenties.

Both have had the life and blood nearly sucked out of them. Ryan walks towards the man and notices he is no longer breathing and has no pulse. Ryan says in a calm expression and pretends to be shocked as he jests," Huh dead."

Ryan looks over towards the woman and scolds her, "It is such a shame you and your man turned out to be vagrants. If it is one thing the Vasiles cannot tolerate are common thieves. That and poor manners. Which is why you were made to suffer a slow agonizing death rather a quick death."

The woman, who can barely breathe or speak mutters the words while gasping for air," Please, please let me go. It was my father who made us do it."

Ryan looks at her with disdain and then a twisted smile and says," Don't worry about your father, the carriage driver. I took care of him earlier this evening. To think he sent you two to rob us so he could retire in luxury."

Ryan pauses for a minute and says, "Well, it does appear you have learned your lesson. Therefore, I will free you. Free you from your worthless existence."

With those words fangs appear from Ryan's mouth and his eyes turn blood red. Ryan looks at his female victim's neck which is perforated with bite marks all around.

Ryan, who is a vampire gets on his knees and bites the woman in her thigh, puncturing her skin with his fangs. Ryan begins to suck the remaining amount of blood from the woman, who is too tired to even scream. After a few minutes of Ryan ravaging her upper thigh, the woman breathes her last breath and dies. Ryan stands up with blood dripping from his mouth as he lets out a growl.

CHAPTER 3

Margaret is relaxing in the tub as she is fully reclined. The lather of the bath soap covers her glistening skin and eases the tension of her body. A knock is heard at the door. Countess Mariana Vasile's voice is heard saying," Miss Margaret, may I enter."

" Yes, you may enter, Countess Vasile", replies Margaret. Countess Vasile enters the room carrying some towels and a nightgown. She admires Margret's beauty, her wet dark auburn hair and the sight of her silky skin which is partially exposed.

Countess Vasile says, "I brought you some towels and a night gown you can wear tonight."

Margaret, who is normally modest and shy about her body as she is a virgin, seems comfortable with Countess Vasile in the room with her and says calmly with gratitude," That is so nice of you, my Countess."

Countess Vasile replies with a hospitable smile, "Please, you may call me Mariana."

Margaret responds," As you wish, Mariana and you can just address me as Margaret."

Mariana looks towards the glass double doors and sees her husband, Bogdan, peering in from the outside. Margaret stands up in the tub giving a full view of her round ass towards Bogdan, who is certainly impressed by the site.

Mariana helps Margaret out of the tub and begins drying her off with a towel and asks," Margaret, if I may inquire a personal question, have you been touched by your soon to be husband or any other man for that matter?

Margaret thinks that is such an odd question for her to be asked? Mariana notices Margaret is embarrassed and apologizes, "Oh please forgive me. Where are my manners?"

Margaret replies, "No it is all right. I am a virgin. My Bruce wants to wait until our wedding night."

Mariana replies," I see. Is your Bruce a virgin as well?" Margaret replies," He says he is." Mariana nods her head with doubt.

There is a brief awkward silence and Margaret covers herself with a towel. Mariana says," My dear Margaret, you are such a beautiful young woman. What if I told you, there is a way you can keep your beauty forever and have eternal life."

Margaret, who is both puzzled and intrigued asks," Thank for the compliment as you are beautiful as well, Mariana, but how would that be possible? That is eternal life?"

Mariana motions toward the terrace door and says," Let my husband, Bogdan explain." Bogdan enters the room abruptly from the terrace and asks Margaret," What do you know of vampires my dear?"

"Vampires?", Margaret responds with astonishment." Creatures that can only come out at night and feed on the blood of the living. At least that is what I have been told."

Bogdan responds," That is mostly true, but I would like to think we are more evolved than just mere creatures."

After hearing Bogdan's response, Margaret feels a sense of fear inside of her as she backs away from both Bogdan and Mariana and asks," You mean to say you are vampires?", as Margaret takes a deep breath.

Bogdan replies, "Yes, my dear. I have walked this earth for nearly three hundred seventy years and my lovely bride, Mariana just celebrated her two hundredth birthday."

Mariana adds, "Ryan is a vampire as well but only at the age of a hundred and three. We are not the monsters you hear about in folklore. Though sometimes we must do monstrous things in order to survive."

Feeling frantic and vulnerable as she is naked except for the towel that is covering her, Margaret looks over towards the full body mirror where both Bogdan and Mariana are standing in front of, but their reflections are not seen. It is as if they are not there. She is stunned and scared and realizes that Bogdan and Mariana are vampires.

Margaret who feels tense and anxious asks," But you kill people, and you mean to kill me as well?"

Bogdan replies and assures Margaret," It is true. We do sometimes kill people, normally those who wish us harm. But mortals kill each other all of the time, whether it is for land, money, resources, or domination. We kill for survival and not every person we feed on dies necessarily. We do not wish to kill you. We wish to make you a part of our family."

Mariana adds," Ever so often we meet someone we deem worthy and make them one of our children by converting them from a mortal to a vampire, thus being immortal. We did this with Ryan many decades ago as we have with several others. All living across Europe and some have even left for America. Now we would like you to join us."

Bogdan in a persuasive voice," Just think you will be immortal. You will never age one day. You will have a power and knowledge that no mortal can possess. The only negative, you will never be able to walk in the sunlight again or bear children."

Margaret who is stunned but answers," I don't know what to say. Part of me is horrified by the thought. Yet I am, also, captivated by your offer. But what about my Bruce, who I mean to marry?"

Scoffing, Mariana retorts," Oh please. Does he really love you or does he just want you to be a vessel to bear his children? Will he treat you like a princess or just a possession, he can keep under control?"

"Sure, you will have to be obedient towards us. But I assure you. You will have more freedom and power than you can possibly imagine. Forgot your Bruce. Besides, I can tell you are smitten with Ryan. You can be with him every night. You will have the ability to seduce and hypnotize any man or woman from now till forever", convincingly, Bogdan states.

Margaret thinks to herself as she looks around the room. She looks at Count and Countess Vasile with confusion and shock by their words and their offer. Margaret feels a nauseous sensation in her stomach, as if she may get sick.

At the same time, she feels lust in her heart and a wanting need to be someone else, someone who is strong, confident, and uninhibited in her thoughts and her actions. For her entire twenty years on this earth, she has lived the way her parents wanted, the way the church wants and what society wants and dictates.

Margaret is really not sure if she even loves Bruce as this is to be an arranged marriage. With a sense of fear and angst, Margaret asks," What of my family? What about Bruce and his family? They will surely come looking for me."

Bogdan replies," We have our ways to get them off your scent. Don't worry, we will not harm them if that is your wish."

"We will be your family and your mentors", declares Mariana. "In time we will teach you how to harness your powers. How to feed? How to defend yourself, how to kill if necessary and how to love in the vampire way. Eventually, you can choose to stay here with us or live elsewhere expanding our family. Either way you will always be connected to us."

Margaret makes her decision and confidently says," I want all of that. I can't explain why, but I feel this is where I belong. What do I need to do?"

Bogdan steps towards Margaret and says," There is a process. An initiation, an initiation of blood."

Mariana adds," Bogdan and I will feed on you. We will drink your blood but not all. Then you will drink our blood. Once that has happened you will become one of us."

Margaret, whose fear as turned to determination, says," Shall we begin."

Bogdan stands in front of Margaret and stairs into her eyes. Margaret stairs back into Bogdan's intoxicating eyes, which change color from brown to blood red. Margaret begins to feel lightheaded as if she was floating in the air.

Mariana discards Margaret's towel and tosses it on the floor while whispering in Margaret's ear," Don't fight it. Just relax and embrace it."

Bogdan walks behind Margaret and fangs begin to form from Bogdan's teeth. Mariana's eyes turn red as well and fangs appear from her mouth. From behind Bogdan bites firmly in Margaret's neck. Margaret gasps in pain and fear.

Then Mariana sinks her teeth into the other side of Margaret's neck. The young Scottish lass feels a sharp pain starting from her neck and spreading throughout her body. She does not cry or scream but stays silent. She sees her bedroom which appears to be covered in blood. She wonders if this sensation is this real or is he just imagining the blood pouring down the walls of the room and running across the floor. The jagged arduous pain now has turned into a state of euphoria and ecstasy. Margaret has never felt such a feeling and hopes and wishes for it to become more intense.

The Vasiles release their bite on Margaret and lay her on the bed on her back as blood drips from their mouths.

Bogdan unveils a dagger and makes a slice on Mariana's right forearm. Mariana takes the dagger from Bogdan and slices his left forearm.

The Count and Countess walk toward Margaret who sits up. Bogdan says to her," Taste our blood, combine it with yours and become one with us."

Margaret does not hesitate and begins sucking and drinking the blood from both Bogdan and Mariana. At first, she feels nauseated and hears the screams and cries of Count and Countess Vasiles' many victims. The sick feeling in her has transformed to a feeling of empowerment as blood now drips from her lips. She lies all the way back on the bed. Margaret's eyes begin to turn from blue to yellow and begins to moan.

She looks and sees Bogdan and Mariana undressing. Until this night, Margret has never looked at a woman in a sexual manner. She lusts over Mariana's large breasts. She glances over to Bogdan and admires his muscular structure and almost erect shaft.

Mariana begins gently biting on Margaret's inner thigh before licking and nibbling on Margaret's pussy. The feeling in her area is a feeling she couldn't possibly imagine. Out of pure instinct she reaches and grabs Bagdon's cock and strokes it before pleasuring him orally.

After reaching a full erection, Bogdan gets behind his vampire bride, Mariana, who is on all fours and continuing to pleasure Margaret. He thrusts his hardness inside Mariana, who moans passionately. Margaret eyes now go from yellow to red and fangs begin to appear. Margaret has now turned into a vampire and all three participants in the initiation of blood orgasm simultaneously.

Bogdan and Mariana step back and smile. Margaret who looks back at the Count and Countess and smiles deviously. Her transformation from a meek mortal to a powerful vampire is now complete.

Mariana, whose long black hair reaches all the way down her back says," You are one of us now. Let's us offer you a gift."

Margaret replies," You have given me eternal life and youth along with my first orgasm. What more could you give me, my Count and Countess?"

Bogdan lifts his hand and the bedroom door leading to the hallway opens and Ryan emerges and enters the room.

Margaret is surprised and pleased as Ryan returns the look of glee. Bogdan and Mariana leave the room as Bogdan turns toward Ryan and says," She is all yours." Bogdan and Mariana take their leave as the bedroom door slams shut.

TALE 2: ARMAND AND ELENA

CHAPTER 1

It is a frosty winter night in the city of Chicago, Illinois. The evening is cold just above freezing with a few inches of snow covering the whole downtown area. The streets are clear, and snowplows are seen removing the remains of frigid slush and white powder from the sky.

Downtown Chicago is somewhat sluggish with patrons gathering at their favorite restaurant or tavern this evening. A sharp contrast from the previous night which was New Year's Eve where every establishment in the downtown area, whether on Rush Street, Dearborn Street or Michigan Avenue and all places in between were jammed pack with patrons celebrating the end of 2014 and the beginning of 2015.

One such establishment, Smitty's Bar, where just a few patrons gather inside. An older gentleman named Stan is sitting at the end of the bar who is a bit intoxicated and is reciting the entire history of the American Civil War to the bartender, Will. "Let me tell you Will about General Stonewall Jackson."

There are two couples in their thirties sitting at a nearby table. All four of whom are trying not to laugh as Stan continues analyzing the battle tactics of General Stonewall Jackson.

A group of three college aged young men are seen in the back playing pool. Meanwhile a man named Armand Gerhart, about thirty years of age is sitting at the opposite end of the bar. The dark haired and dark complected dashing fellow takes a sip of his mug which is now half full of draft beer.

Armand is of German descent on his father's side and his mother immigrated from Spain. At the age of seven his mother abandoned him and his father, which left Armand, who is an only child without a mother figure.

His father, who worked long hours at the local slaughterhouse, would never remarry, opting to bed several women over the course of Armand's childhood. Armand was forced to be self-reliant and raise himself. To bury his past as a youth, Armand would distance himself from his father and the rest of his family as he preferred to only rely and trust himself.

Looking up at the row of televisions that sit above the bar, Armand notices one of the televisions is playing the end of the Rose Bowl game between Michigan State and Stanford. But the television with the hockey game has caught the man's attention as the hometown Chicago Blackhawks are playing the Montreal Canadians. The excitable announcer of the game is loudly audible in the background, 'Kane takes the pass from Toews, he shoots and scores. Chicago takes a 3 to 1 lead with a powerplay goal from Patrick Kane.' The thrilled patrons in the bar begins to cheer their hometown hockey team.

*****

A few blocks away from Smitty's, a young French-Canadian woman by the name of Elena Durand is exiting Mastro's Steakhouse. Elena is a chef at the steakhouse, whose shift is over for the night.

Elena who comes from a large middle-class family in Canada is the middle child of five children with an older brother and sister and two younger brothers.

She was always encouraged by her parents to pursue whatever career she wanted. As she would often help her mother in preparing meals at home, Elena would develop a glowing passion for cooking and would dream of becoming a chef. To pursue her enthusiasm for cooking and would attend one of the top culinary schools in the world in Chicago.

She would have preferred to attend such a school in Paris or Tuscany but was unable to afford such a venture but was grateful for the opportunity to attend such a fine institute no matter where it was located.

After finishing school should gain her citizenship in the United States and now holds the position of an executive chef at the infamous Mastro's Steakhouse.

Looking up towards the sky, Elena marvels at the snow as it has just begun to fall from the sky again. She also sighs as she is fatigued from working every night for the past several evenings. Even though she has a car, most of the time Elena elects to walk to her apartment, which is three blocks away. Often times it is faster to walk to work than to drive in the traffic.

Elena, who has dirty blond hair that is kept in a ponytail, covers her head with a beanie and puts on her gloves. She begins walking towards the direction of her apartment building as she can detect the smell of frigid moisture in the air which is also smacking her from the breeze from nearby Lake Michigan.

The streets in downtown Chicago are quiet this Wednesday evening. Elena crosses the street and walks another block as she walks past Smitty's bar. She stops and glances at the bar as she was just there the previous night celebrating the new year.

Elena grins but continues walking and takes a turn down an alley, which she uses as a short cut to arrive at her apartment. The alley has a few lights on each side. One for every building.

Strolling nonchalantly down the alley, Elena hears the sound of what she suspects is a big bird flapping its wings. Elena with a pondered look on her face stares upward and sees nothing, she thinks to herself,' Surely that couldn't be a bird. It would have migrated south by now. But what could it be?'

Walking a little faster down the alley, Elena comes to a sudden stop as she notices a silhouette of what might be a person.

The young cook can see her breath escape her mouth as she shivers from the cold. She reaches into her purse, where she keeps a taser. Elena shouts out in her French-Canadian accent," Hello. Who are you?"

The figure at the end of the alley says nothing, takes a few steps toward Elena, and stops. "Whoever you are. You should know that I'm armed!", shouts Elena.

The silent figure begins walking towards Elena at a steady pace. Elena is now scared and does not know if she has the courage to stand up to this potential attacker.

She begins to back up slowly as her heart begins to pound. She wonders if the taser which she has never used will even work on this stalker. Elena then turns quickly as she plans to run in the opposite direction.

As Elena turns, she bumps into a young woman who must have been standing right behind her. The young woman says in a Scottish accent," Oh pardon me. I didn't me to startle you."

Elena responds frantically," Yes pardon me", as Elena runs towards the opposite end of the alley.

The young woman scratches her head and begins twirling her auburn hair and says," What an odd woman."

A voice from a man also with a Scottish accent is heard behind her saying," Well Margaret you let another get away."

Margaret replies, "Oh please, Ryan. She was hardly our type. She was too innocent.

Ryan replies," I know you are a better judge of character than I am. But I do love a good scare."

"Well, you sure scared the hell out of her." answers Margaret, who pauses and marvels at the weather and says, "I do love the winter in Chicago."

Both Ryan and Margaret hear a clicking sound behind them. Then they hear a man's voice in a commanding tone say," Ok turn around right now both of you."

Ryan and Margaret turn as they see two men, one tall and the other short, both holding switchblade knives in their hands. Ryan replies sarcastically, "Wow those are some cute little knives you have. Compensating for something?"

The taller of the two robbers says with disgust," Enough funny talk asshole. Both of you give us your wallets, and jewelry and maybe we won't gut you both."

Margaret smiling in jest responds," Ah, I love a man who talks dirty", she says with a smirk and then winks at both the robbers.

The shorter thief says in a stern and annoyed voice," Listen bitch, we are going to count to three."

Ryan interrupts," Can you even count that high?" he says while laughing.

The taller thief yells, "That is it! We are going to count to three and if you don't hand over your valuables, we are going to show you your own blood."

Margaret with her dark cold eyes smirks and says in a scolding manor, "Blood, you dare use that word in our presence. Go ahead and count you dumb cunts."

Both the thieves are shocked by Margaret's defiance, but the shorter robber says, "One!" Then both Margaret's and Ryan's eyes shift to red. The taller thief who is shivering from the cold says, "Two!" Ivory white fangs form and begin to grow from both Ryan and Margaret's mouth.

Both Ryan and Margaret look at the two robbers who are now trembling in fear. Ryan says to them laughing with an evil smile, "Three."

Ryan grabs the taller thief by the throat and with one hand lifts the robber up in the air who is petrified and shocked by Ryan's superhuman strength. Ryan presses the him up against a brick wall as he grasps the taller thief's throat who is unable to make a sound.

Meanwhile, the shorter thief tries to make a run for it, but Margaret jumps on his back like a hyena. With one grasping motion she rips into the derelict's throat and pulls out his larynx and discards it.

Margaret opens her mouth wide and thrusts towards the shorter thief's open wound as the victim falls to the ground with Margaret still latched onto him. Her fangs sink into his throat and begins drinking away his blood.

Ryan, who has slammed the taller robber up against the brick wall several times with his one hand like a battering ram, lowers the robber to the ground and twists the taller robber's head a hundred and eighty degrees. Ryan opens his mouth wide showing his fangs and bites into the back of the taller thief's neck. While sucking the blood out of his victim's neck, Ryan bites off a chunk of flesh and spits it out.

After sucking most of the blood out of the shorter robber, Margaret rips the robber's arms and legs off and begins sucking any blood that's left and starts gnawing on the body parts.

Slicing the tall robber's head right off, Ryan gleams devilishly and tosses the decapitated head in the air and punts the head like a football as he laughs.

Looking over towards Margaret, who is still feasting on the other unfortunate thief's limbs, Ryan asks with a sarcastic smile," Want any buffalo wing sauce with those."

Margaret looks at Ryan, who has bitten into the taller robbers lower spinal column, and responds, "No, this fat motherfucker tastes just fine." She then asks while giggling," Do you wants some salt with yours?"

Ryan replies chuckling," No, my doctor wants me to cut down on the sodium."

After Margaret and Ryan finish devouring the unfortunate thieves, they both look at each other and smile. They embrace and begin kissing one another. The feeding of blood both sustains their hunger but also arouses them.

For the past couple hundred years this duo of vampires have been inseparable like two twins as they enjoying hunting together. But they have also developed a lustful bond built on mutual attraction and respect.

Margaret whispers in a seductive voice, "I think we need to get back to our hotel." They both without hesitation transform into two bats and fly off gracefully to their next destination.

CHAPTER 2

Still running from the alley, Elena finally slows down, pauses, and takes a deep breath. Whatever or whoever she encountered in the alley filled her with pure dread and fear like she had never felt before.

Elena begins to calm down as she looks behind her and sees no one following her. She begins to shiver as her nose is wet and runny.

Smitty's Bar is right in front of her with its big green and red neon sign. Elena figures she could use a drink and enters the establishment.

As Elena enters Smitty's she notices it is not terribly busy at all. She sits down in the middle of the bar and can hear Stan telling the bartender, Will, every detail of the battle at Gettysburg.

Will tells Stan, "Hold on one second, Stan. Let me help this lady." Will walks over to Elena and asks, "What can I get you, miss?"

Still a bit disturbed from her encounter in the alley, Elena answers," A gin and tonic, please."

"One gin and tonic coming right up", says Will. As Will makes the drink he asks Elena, "You were here last night, weren't you?"

"Yes. Some friends from work and me. You actually remember. It was pretty busy last night?" answers Elena.

Will replies," I'm a bartender it's my job to remember." Will hands Elena the drink and says," That will be five dollars.

Elena reaches in her purse and hands Will seven dollars and says," Keep the change." Will says," Thanks", as he walks back over to Stan.

Staring up towards one of the televisions, Elena notices the hockey game and sees that Chicago has defeated Montreal by the score of three to one. "Awe damn" says Elena in a disappointed voice.

"Not a hockey fan?" asks Armand who is still at the bar and sitting three chairs away from Elena.

Elena turns and looks at Armand and is surprised and taken off guard by his good looks. Not the type of guy she would expect to see in a bar late night in the middle of the week. She answers Armand, "I like hockey just fine except when my team loses."

Armand, also, happens to be struck by Elena's natural beauty. Even if she has just finished work and is not all made up, she is still incredibly attractive. Armand asks," I take it you are not a Blackhawks fan. Listening to your accent, you must be a Canadian's fan. Let me guess you're from somewhere in the Quebec province?"

Elena responds sarcastically," Well you're perceptive. Who are you the great detective, Sherlock Holmes?'

"Actually, my name is Armand, but I am a private investigator. "Maybe not as great as Sherlock Homes but I do well", responds Armand with a confident look.

Elena smiles and replies," Well then Armand, my name is Elena, and to answer your question. Yes, I am from the Montreal area but lived most of my teenage years in Nova Scotia." Elena continues to say," Yes, I've been a Canadians fan since I was eight when my parents took me to my first game."

"I admire your loyalty to your team. Loyalty is an important quality for anyone to have" replies Armand, who then asks," So what made you move to Chicago?"

Elena responds a question of her own," How do you know I moved here, and I am not simply visiting?"

"Because, more than likely if you were visiting, a young woman such as yourself, I'm guessing you are about twenty- three, would not be visiting this city, alone. Plus, I see you are wearing a chef's uniform under you coat. Which tells me that not only do you live here, but you also work here as a chef, more than likely Mastros as I can smell the aroma of a nice cut of ribeye on you."

"Well, you are definitely a private investigator, all right. I do live here in Chicago", responds Elena while being amazed with Armand's intelligence and then answers, "I came here to attend Culinary School. After graduating, I thought about returning to Canada but the culinary scene in Chicago is thriving, so I decided to stay."

Armand moves down the bar to sit closer to Elena and asks, "So was it difficult finding a job here?"

"It wasn't too difficult. I have been working at Mastros since back when I was attending school. After I graduated a year ago, they made me executive chef", answers Elena.

"That's impressive," says Armand as he gazes into Elena's hazel-colored eyes. He then asks, "So what are your long-term goals? Do you want your own restaurant?"

Elena, who notices Armand's glance and is somewhat intrigued by his curiosity, answers," Either own a restaurant or maybe run a catering service." Elena pauses for a moment as she finishes her drink and asks," What about you? Do you have your own agency?"

"Actually, I just now started my own agency," answers Armand, who continues to say," I started as a bail bonds agent. Then was hired by an investigation agency and finally was able to save enough money to start my own business."

Armand then asks Elena," I see your drink is empty. Can I buy you another drink?"

Elena responds," Sure but don't think that means I'm going to sleep with you."

Looking stunned and feeling speechless, Armand replies," Oh ok. I wasn't really going to go there."

With embarrassment Elena responds," I'm sorry that was rude and presumptive of me. It's just that, I haven't had the best luck with men recently."

"Will, can you bring a gin and tonic to the lady and another beer for me? Put it on my tab," Armand asks politely towards Will. He then responds to Elena," It is ok.

I haven't had much luck with women." Armand also asks," You do seem a little tense. Is there something else bothering you?"

Elena responds," Something happened while I was walking home, that freaked me out." After a pause, Elena continues," I don't live far from the restaurant and always take a short cut down this alley. I saw a person standing in the shadows. He was just staring at me and wouldn't speak. It was so creepy and nerve racking. Then I bumped into this weird lady who startled the hell out of me. That is when I ran into here."

Scratching his head, Armand replies," Sounds like a woman and man robbery team. It is common in most big cities. The woman distracts the target while the man surprises them, and they rob their victim." Armand continues," You should really avoid walking down alleys at night or just drive."

Elena responds," I have taken that route for two years and never had a problem. I have a car. It's just easier and quicker to walk because of Chicago traffic. But I suppose you might be right."

*****

An hour has passed. Armand and Elena have had a few more drinks and have taken the time to get to know one another. They talked quite a bit and laughed at each other's stories.

Elena who is smiling but still exhausted says, "Well, I do need to get home. Thank you for your company. I feel more relaxed than I did when I entered here."

"You are welcome. It was my pleasure.," replies Armand who, also, asks," Do you need a ride home?"

"Normally, I would say no but given what happened earlier. I will take you up on your offer," answers Elena.

Armand pays his tab and he and Elena exit Smitty's. As they walk outside, the snow has stopped falling but both of them notice several police cars and an ambulance with their lights on.

The vehicles are parked by the alley where hours earlier Elena had fled desperately from. The police officers are blocking off the alley with barricades and caution tape.

"I wonder what the fuck is going on there," wonders Armand and asks Elena, "Is it ok, if we go over there to see what's happening? Elena responds, "Sure, I am kind of curious as well."

Armand sees one of the detectives who are at the crime scene and approaches him and asks, "Hey Mike, what happened?"

Looking stunned, Mike looks over to Armand and says, "Hi Armand, where did you come from?"

Armand replies," I was over at Smitty's and saw the scene over here. What's wrong, Mike, you look like you just witnessed Armageddon."

Mike looks back at Armand and answers somberly," Perhaps I have. We discovered two mutilated bodies in that alley. Both male and both ripped apart."

"Sweet Jesus!", Armand responds in a stunned manner." What could have done that? A wild animal?" asks Armand.

"In downtown Chicago, In the middle of the winter? not unless a polar bear escaped out of the zoo?" responds Mike, who then states. "The fucking thing is there should have been blood all over the alley but hardly any at the scene. It is like something sucked all their blood and ripped them apart like a coyote ripping apart chickens."

As she hears the conversation between Armand and Mike, Elena begins to get queasy with terror. She thinks to herself, how just a few hours ago, she was in the alley and could have easily been one of those unfortunate victims.

As Elena stands in horror. Both her and Armand, observe a couple of the ambulance paramedics carrying a black bag over to the ambulance, when one of the paramedics slips on some ice dropping the bag and spilling body parts on the ground including a human head that belonged to one of the thieves, who had attempted to rob Margaret and Ryan a few hours ago.

The gruesome site startles Armand and Elena. Mike looks over and yells over to the paramedics," god damnit, zip that fucking bag up next time."

Armand looks at Elena, then Mike and says," Well, I need to be going. Giving this young Lady a ride home."

"I don't suppose either one of you saw or heard anything," asks Mike. "No, I didn't," answers Armand. "Me neither," answers Elena. "Well, then take care. I will see you later, Armand" says Mike.

*****

A few minutes later, a black Ford Explorer is seen pulling up to an apartment building a few blocks from the horrific murder scene in the alley. The Explorer is being driven by Armand, who shifts the vehicle in park.

Elena is sitting in the passenger seat up front in the vehicle and says to Armand, "Thank you for the ride. Also, thank you for not saying anything to that detective. After all, I was in that alley where those people were killed."

Armand nods his head and replies," Actually the thought never crossed my mind. Besides, it's not like you saw any ferocious beasts in that alley."

Elena has a nervous smile on her face. She is smitten with Armand. Not just because of his handsome looks but how he behaves. She admires the confidence and generosity that she perceives him to have.

Armand notices the smile on Elena's face. He too finds her to be one pretty and caring woman. Not necessarily like a fashion model but more like the girl next door, who would look sexy no matter what she wore. He also admires Elena's sense of humor and intelligence.

"So do you mind walking me to my apartment?" Elena asks Armand.

"Not at all. I imagine you are still a little freaked out from the events of tonight," responds Armand.

They both exit the vehicle and walk towards the apartment building, which looks more like a huge house, that has two apartments downstairs and two apartments upstairs.

As they enter the building, they both can smell marijuana smoke emanating from one of the apartments. "Excuse the smell, there is a couple of college kids that live in that apartment. Though I don't know how they can make it through school, smoking as much as they do", explains Elena who is embarrassed by the habits of her neighbors.

Chuckling, Armand replies, "It's all right, I 've partaken in the past myself."

Smiling back at Armand Elena says" Yes me too," as they walk up the staircase leading upstairs to Elena's apartment as Armand follows behind. The staircase leads to a hallway with one apartment on one side and another apartment on the other.

Elena walks towards her left and stops in front of the door to her apartment which has a brass plate on the door in the shape of the number three. She turns around and faces Armand and says, "I guess one good thing from being scared out of my mind in that alley was I got to meet you." Elena then goes to kiss Armand on the lips, who reciprocates the kiss back to Elena.

"So would you like to come in and see my place. If you like you can even stay the night. "If you want to?" asks Elena.

"I thought you said earlier when I bought you that drink, you weren't going to sleep with me.," asks Armand.

"Who said anything about sleeping?" replies Elena with a sly smile on her face. Elena unlocks the door and both she and Armand enter the apartment and Elena abruptly shuts the door behind them.

CHAPTER 3

Within a year of their first meeting, Armand and Elena fell in love with each other like two characters in a fairy tale. and were married. Their relationship was very passionate, spending most of their spare time together as they enjoyed each other's company.

As both Armand and Elena were both career driven, they decided not to have children. When they were not spending time together, both were intently committed to their careers.

Elena would eventually start her own catering business. She would provide catering to many conventions held in the United States and Canada.

Armand's private investigation agency would continue to flourish. He would earn the reputation of one of the elite private investigators in the Midwestern part of the United States.

It is now November of 2024 in. Armand and Elena have become quite successful financially. However, the once burning flames that fueled their passion for one another has begun to flicker and has nearly died off. Their love is only a small fragment of what it once was. They have become as distant as two separate coasts and as frigid as a Chicago winter.

It is a cool damp autumn morning in Chicago. The odor of damp leaves that have changed color and fallen to the ground can be sniffed in the chilly air.

Years ago, shortly after they married, Armand and Elena purchased a home in one of the more affluent neighborhoods in Chicago.

Armand is sitting in the spacious and ceramic tiled kitchen. He is sitting at the breakfast nook eating some oatmeal while viewing the news on his laptop.

Elena walks into the kitchen. Armand and her glance at each other as Armand says nonchalantly," good morning honey,"

"Good morning, dear," responds Elena unenthusiastically, and opens the refrigerator door and bends over to reach some orange juice.

Armand admires her from where he is sitting. Elena is just wearing a T-shirt and blue jeans. Despite the distance between them, Armand still finds his wife attractive and is determined to make things right.

"So how was your trip to Austin?" asks Armand, as Elena had just returned from a catering job in Austin, Texas for a special convention.

"It went really well," replies Elena. She then asks Armand," How was your business trip for your client in San Diego?"

Armand replies," It was productive. I found out quite a bit of information for my client. She didn't like hearing the information, but she needed and wanted to hear it."

"Well, that is why they pay you the big bucks, I suppose.," responds Elena.

Standing up abruptly from his seat Armand says," Look honey, I know things haven't been the same between us for quite some time. I want to try to change that."

Armand reveals a gold bracelet that is sparkling with red rubies and hands it to Elena and says to her," I bought you this while I was in San Diego."

"Wow it's beautiful," says Elena in a stunned voice. Elena is taken by surprise as it has been several years since her husband has bought her a gift outside of her birthday, Christmas, or their wedding anniversary. She then states," But this isn't going to fix us overnight."

"I know but it's a start. A fresh start, I hope", Armand says gleefully. "There is more. We need to take a vacation. I found the perfect place."

Elena asks with a curious look," Where would that be?" Armand replies," An old Scottish castle. You have always said you would love to stay at an old European castle."

"Where did you get this idea?", Elena asks," You are not the type of person who just jumps into something."

"This time I am. My client told me about this exclusive New Year's Eve party they have at this castle, named Castle Vasile, named after the Romanian family who settled there centuries ago. So, as a bonus she offered to pay for our trip."

Elena smiles nervously as she is startled by this news. She wonders what has changed with Armand, but she doesn't want to disappoint him and replies with fraudulent excitement," That is wonderful. Maybe you are right dear. Maybe we just need to get away for a few days and enjoy ourselves like we used to."

"I knew you would like the idea. We will leave on the 30th. We fly into Edinburgh then spend the night there. The next morning, we take a train to Kirkcaldy where the castle is," says Armand with excitement. Who, also, says, "There is one catch. Since this is a private and exclusive party, we can't tell anyone else about where we are going. The owners of the castle like their privacy."

Elena smiles and begins to relax. She thinks to herself that this might actually be fun, but she questions with apprehension whether she still loves Armand, and does he even still love her or are they just going through tedious motions?

CHAPTER 4

It is the afternoon of December 31, 2024, in Scotland not far from the city of Kirkaldy. The clouds are grey with a few rays of sunlight trying to peak through the clouds.

Snow has covered the countryside and the scent of salt from the nearby ocean fills the air. In the background stands Castle Vasile, overlooking the ocean. The exterior of the castle has not changed much in centuries as it still sits on a small island surrounded by water with a bridge made of stone connecting the castle to land. The bridge has since been widened and repaved to allow automobiles to arrive at the castle.

A yellow taxicab crosses the bridge as it drives to the main circle driveway in front of the entrance to the castle. Inside the circle driveway stands a statue of a being that appears to be half human and half gargoyle or perhaps a demon.

The taxicab parks and the driver exits the vehicle and opens the back door allowing the passengers to exit the vehicle.

The passengers are Armand and Elena, who arrived in Scotland yesterday and now have arrived at Castle Vasile for the exclusive New Year's Eve party.

The driver opens the truck of the taxi and hands Armand and Elena their luggage as Armand pays the driver in cash.

A look of awe and amazement engulfs both Armand's and Elena's faces as they take a long look at the impressive and gothic exterior of the castle.

"This is astonishing, Armand," remarks Elena who is awestruck by the castles and the beautiful winter scenery of Scotland.

With a confident smile, Armand replies, "Yes, it is something like out of a book or movie. I knew you would like it. Let's see what the inside of it looks like."

Both Armand and Elena tread towards the front entrance which has two black wooden double doors that is accentuated by the light grey stone masonry of the exterior of the castle.

There is a doorbell which was installed a few decades ago. Armand presses the doorbell and moments later the double door opens.

Opening the doors is Argyle, the loyal ghoul who has served the Vasile's for centuries, but as far as Armand and Elena would guess maybe a couple of decades as Argyle looks to be in his late fifties.

Argyle greets the couple with a stoic look on his face and says with a thick Scottish accent," Good afternoon, how may I help you."

Armand replies," Yes, we are here for the New Year's Eve gathering. Madam Lillith invited us. Here is our invitation." Armand hands Argyle the invitation.

Argyle looks over the invitation and then looks up at both Armand and Elena and says, "Of course you must be Mr. and Mrs. Gerhart. Madam Lillith spoke very highly of you both. Please come in."

As Armand and Elena enter the front foyer there are astonished by the tapestries and decorations. There are a few paintings of gargoyles, batts, and wolves. The fresh aroma of incense dominates the air within the castle.

Elena who is admiring the interior of the castle says," I am sure this would be a terrific place to host a Halloween party."

Argyle replies," Oh the Count and Countess host an annual Halloween event every year, but it is mostly for family and remarkably close friends. The Vasiles celebrate Halloween in a comparable way, you Americans celebrate Thanksgiving."

Armand looks at his watch which shows the time to be two o'clock and asks," We aren't too early are we? Has Madam Lillith arrived yet?"

Argyle responds," Madam Lillith was here earlier but had an important engagement to attend but she will be returning around six o' clock. And you are not too early at all. Another couple have arrived, and we are awaiting another couple, also from America. May I interest you in a snack or perhaps some lunch?"

Elena replies," We had lunch before leaving Edinburgh so I'm not hungry.

Armand confirms Elena's statement by saying," Yes, I think we would just like to relax in our room until tonight festivities."

Argyle replies, "Of course Mr. and Mrs. Gerhart, I will have someone help you with your luggage at once. Vincent I am of need of your assistance."

A tall and burly Englishman enters the foyer. Vincent has the looks of a lumberjack but never speaks.

Argyle says," Vincent, I need you to assist our guests with their luggage as we escort them to their room."

Vincent takes both pieces of luggage and follows Argyle, Armand, and Elena upwards the red carpeted spiral staircase that leads to the second level of the castle where most of the guest rooms reside.

As they walk up the staircase, Armand, and Elena view more of the castle with astonishment and surprise.

As they reach the top of the staircase, Elena and Armand follow Argyle as he leads them to their room. Vincent follows them with their luggage.

Argyle states as he opens the door to the guest room," We will be serving drinks and appetizers in our lounge at 6:00." As everyone enters the Gerhart's guestroom. "Dinner will be held at seven o'clock. After dinner there will be drinks and music in the ball room to usher in the new year."

As Vincent places the luggage on the floor by the bed, Armand and Elena look over the room with surprise as the room is quite grand with stone walls covered with many decorations such as large paintings and old Scottish armor and tartans. There is also a whirlpool tub in the center of the room.

"Are the accommodations to your likening?" asks Argyle. "Absolutely!" answers Elena in an enthusiastic tone as she opens the glass double door that leads to the terrace." Armand says," The room is quite nice. Thank you."

"The room has a house phone if you need assistance as the cell phone signals can be a bit unreliable. If you like I can send someone to your room at five o'clock for a tour of the common areas and then escort you to the lounge," says Argyle.

"That would be excellent" answers Armand. "Very well, we will take our leave sir", Argyle replies as he and Victor exit the room.

Armand walks out to the terrace and both he and Elena exchange glances, and both smile at each one another. Perhaps the passion that once existed between the two lovers, can once again be rekindled.

*****

A few hours later the sun sets. Down in the depths of the castle in a murky and gloomy dungeon which has a foul stench of rotted flesh and death. There are five fresh corpses of three males and two females laying on the cold damp floor. All of the corpses have been drained of their blood and have been gutted like stuck pigs.

In the next room there is a small pool built into the floor. On one end sits Bogdan Vasile who has his arm around his voluptuous vampire wife, Mariana Vasile, both have a gold chalice and drinking blood from them.

On the other end of the pool sits Lillith, a female vampire, originally from Italy, who was the first mortal initiated by Bogdan and Mariana transforming her into a vampire. She is also sipping blood out of a gold chalice.

Margaret and Ryan are seen exiting the pool. Shortly after the five vampires awoke, they all took turns feeding on their five victims all of whom were criminals guilty of kidnapping and human trafficking.

As they dry each other off, Margaret says to Bogdan and Mariana, "I suppose Ryan and I will get dressed and go upstairs to greet our guests."

Ryan asks Lillith, "I assume you will be there as well." Lillith responds with delight, "I will be there soon. After all I have two couples that I have invited."

As both Margaret and Ryan dry off and put on their robes, Margaret says," We will see you there Lillith."

Ryan says to Bogdan and Mariana with anticipation," And we will see the both of you at dinner?" Bogdan replies," Of course."

The youthful and energetic Ryan and Margaret, whose personalities and physical features are that of two teenagers leave the dreary pool area as they make their way upstairs to get dressed for tonight's festivities.

Filled with content and blissful feeling as she enjoys having her closest friends around, Mariana says to Lillith, "It is nice having you here with us again Lillith. Even if it is for only a few days."

■■

" You and Bogdan are my closest friends, and it is always a treat feasting on blood together and then on each other," says with a devilish smile."

"Yes, you have always had such great chemistry with Bogdan and me," Mariana responds with a smirk of her own.

"I suppose I should also get ready for our guests," says Lillith who stands up and steps up out of the pool and grabs a towel to dry herself with.

Lillith is built much like her dear mentor, Mariana, with a busty hourglass figure only her entire back and butt are covered with gothic and morbid tattoos that she has collected over the years. Where Mariana has long straight black hair, Lillith has long mahogany brown hair with some curls.

"My Count, my Countess, I will see you at dinner," Lillith says as she cover herself in with a towel and takes her leave.

Bogdan says to Mariana has he drinks the last sip of blood from his chalice," My radiant bride here is to another eventful New Years with my loving and stunning wife."

Mariana responds gleefully, "And to another new Years with my devoted and handsome husband. "The loving couple toast each other with their chalices and kiss each other.

"We have six candidates. I wonder which ones will be worthy and which ones will be dessert," Mariana says with a gleam in her dark hypnotic brown eyes.

*****

It is now ten minutes after six o'clock in the evening on this New Years Eve. Armand and Elena go into the lounge area of the castle. Armand is wearing a black suite with a stone-grey dress shirt with a black tie. Elena is wearing a royal blue full skirt strapless dress.

Over in the corner of the lounge past the massive fireplace, they spot the bar area. Behind the bar, Ryan is making drinks. He is wearing a long white dress shirt with a red bow tie and red suspenders that go with his dark maroon slacks. Standing next to Ryan is Margaret, dressed in a crimson red halter dress.

Sitting at the bar is another married couple, Winston, and Akiko Addison. Winston who is dressed in a peculiar purple suit with a long tail to his suit jacket much; like what you would see men wear in the nineteenth century, is a Jamaican with long dread locks reaching down his back and quite a tall gentleman. His wife, Akiko who is short and petite, is from Japan and like her husband also favors the color purple as she wears a violet purple empire waist dress.

Elena sees how happy all four of them are as they are drinking and laughing with all four of them oozing bliss and delight.

Margaret notices both Armand and Elena and greets them with her playful Scottish accent," Why hello, you must be Mr. and Mrs. Gerhart. Please join us."

As Armand and Elena stride towards the bar and have a seat. Ryan asks in an enthusiastic voice, "What can I get you two lovely people?" Elena in a shy tone answer, "A gin and tonic for me."

The Scotsman, Ryan then turns and asks Armand" And you sir." Armand replies," I will have your finest Scotch Whiskey."

"Great choice my sir," replies Ryan and continues," This bottle here is from 1763. "It's almost as old as I am," Ryan laughs hysterically as everyone else does.

Margaret says," My name is Margaret, and this is my loving lad, Ryan. We both work here for the Vasiles."

"And I am Winston Addison, and this is my lovely wife, Akiko. We are also guests here." Winston announces in an elegant tone.

"My name is Armand Gerhart, and this is my wife Elena" replies Armand as Elena adds," It is nice to meet all of you."

Akiko responds," Likewise, I am sure we are all going to have a lot of fun tonight."

Walking in the lounge ominously, Lillith enters and says with excitement, "Greetings everyone, Happy New Years Eve!!!" Lillith is wearing a tight forest green sheath dress.

"Let me introduce the last of our guests; Kevin and Cheryl Price," announces Lillith.

Immediately, Elena nearly spits out her drink as she is shocked to hear those names. Elena looks over towards Lillith and is astonished to see Kevin and Cheryl enter the lounge.

Kevin is of average height with dark blonde hair and wearing a navy-blue suit and his wife, Cheryl, a meek and petite looking red head is wearing black dress pants with a black and white poke a dot skirt. Cheryl also wears glasses and is surveying the room suspiciously.

Smiling at Elena, Armand asks Elena," Honey are you all right. You almost spit out your whole drink."

Ryan adds," Yes I didn't make it too strong, did I?"

Margaret says," I told you, Ryan you get a little carried away with the booze."

"Oh no," assures Elena," The drink is fine. It just went down the wrong pipe." Elena begins to fake a cough.

Kevin looking overtly towards Elena and Armand with a peculiar look on his face. He looks over towards Winston and Akiko and thinks that they seem like nice people.

His wife, Cheryl asks, "Are you ok sweetie. You look like you have seen a ghost." Kevin responds," Yes, my dear. I think I am still a little jet lagged from our flight."

Lillith then says," Let's get you two up to the bar and introduce you two to everyone and get you some drinks. I know I could use one."

As Kevin and Cheryl follow Lillith to the bar. to Lillith with a glossy smile introduces the Prices to everyone else.

Outside snow begins to fall again and a strong breeze begins to gust and moving the now all around. What shadowy and unforeseen events will unfold on this New Years Eve night at Castle Vasile?

■■

TALE 3: THE CLIENT AND THE CASE

CHAPTER 1

    It is a crisp autumn October afternoon in Chicago. Even though the bright sun is shining, it is also breezy and chilly. A ten-story office building is observed in the downtown area of Chicago. On the seventh floor right by the elevators is an office with the letters printed on the glass door, *Gerhart Investigation Agency*. Inside there is a reception area and two separate offices.

In one of the offices, Armand is sitting at his desk working on his computer where he is finishing some research for a client.

Janine, Armand's assistant lightly taps on his door and says, "Mr. Gerhart, there is a woman here to see you." "Send her in, Janine, "replies Armand.

Walking into Armand's office is a short petite yet radiant lady in her mid-forties with long strawberry red hair. She is wearing glasses and is dressed in professional women's business attire. Despite her professional appearance, the woman is both attractive and appears to have an aura of confidence about her.

"How can I help you ma'am?" asks Armand, who is sizing up this potential client. The lady is a mystery to him as she has a quiet and private disposition.

The woman responds," My name is Cheryl Price, and I may be in need of your service, Mr. Gerhart," says Cheryl, who speaks in a soft but assertive tone.

"Have a seat, Mrs. Price," Armand says as Cheryl sits down. He asks, "What can I help you with Mrs. Price and please you can call me Armand?"

"You may call me Cheryl then. I will get straight to the point. I am suspecting that my husband is having an affair," replies Cheryl.

"I see," responds Armand who is in deep thought and then asks," So, what makes you think your husband is having an affair?"

"Over the last six months, he has been very distant," responds Cheryl, who has a shameful look on her face and continues to say," Whenever I try to engage with him sexually. He turns me down. He often works out of town."

Armand says," Well I know that feeling. May I ask what your husband does for a living and when is the last time you had sex with him. If that isn't too personal of a question?"

Cheryl's face is as red as her hair as she was not expecting to be asked such a question regarding her sex life. The walls of her apparent confidence begin to tumble, and she now appears vulnerable and hurt. But she gains her composure as she realizes that since she suspects infidelity, asking about her last time with her husband would be a valid question.

"It has been since last December since we had sex. As far as what he does for a living, he manages those silly horror conventions all over North America. Maybe you have heard of them; The Scare-a Cons," Cheryl replies.

Armand thinks to himself, 'That's interesting. Elena has a catering contract with those conventions.' He replies," I have heard of those. May I ask what you do for a living? I can tell by your attire; you are not a housewife."

"I have my own real estate company that I purchased from my parents in St. Louis," answers Cheryl.

"You are from St. Louis, and you came all the way up to Chicago?" asks Armand with an inquisitive expression.

"I wanted the best investigator I could hire, and you were referred to by Mr. Gerald Connor," answers Cheryl, who also, says," I dressed in my work attire so my husband wouldn't suspect anything. As far as he knows I am at work. Not that he cares anyway."

"That is pretty smart of you and yes, I do remember the fraud case that Mr. Connor hired me for," replies Armand who asks," How long have you been married, and do you have children with your husband?"

"We have been married for twenty-three years and we have two grown children both in college. Our son is a junior at the University of Missouri and our daughter is a freshman at Kansas University" answers Cheryl.

Armand studies Cheryl and determines she is sincere and that her suspicions are probably valid and asks "Would you like something to drink, coffee, tea, water? "Cheryl replies, "Tea would be fine."

As Armand makes some tea from Keurig maker in the corner of his office he asks, "So, you believe whenever your husband goes out of town for these conventions, he is hooking up with random women at each of these cities?"

"Yes, I am sure it is unlikely that Kevin, that's his name, is just hooking up with just one woman. Must be a different one in each city. He is quite the charmer."

Cheryl looks around the office and tears emerge from her eyes. Armand hears Cheryl whimpering as she clearly is in pain. Armand brings her a handkerchief and comforts Cheryl by saying, "I know it is difficult but the sooner I can find out what's going on the better."

"We had such a strong marriage and for it to just fall apart, is heartbreaking," cries Cheryl as she wipes the tears from her face."

Armand brings and cup of hot tea and hands it to Cheryl. Cheryl takes a sip and says," Thank you, this isn't bad for tea that comes from a Keurig."

"You are welcome, Cheryl. "Now when is the next weekend that Kevin has a convention?" asks Armand.

Cheryl takes another sip of tea and pulls a pack of cigarettes out of her purse. She asks," May I smoke?

"Sure," answers Armand, who hands Cheryl an ashtray. Cheryl lights up her cigarette and takes a deep drag and almost inhales half the cigarette while Armand lights a cigarette for him as well.

Cheryl answers Armand's question by stating," Not this weekend but next weekend, Kevin has a convention in Las Vegas. He will probably arrive there Thursday night and be there until Sunday evening, perhaps as late as Monday morning."

"Las Vegas, sin city how fitting" says Armand who asks," Do you know what hotel he is staying at?"

"He is staying at the Plaza, which is, also, where the convention is being held."

"I am familiar with Vegas. The Plaza is in the downtown area and is a smaller hotel which will make it easier to locate your husband and monitor him."

Cheryl hands Armand an envelope full of cash. Armand takes the envelope and looks inside. Cheryl asks, "Will that be enough?

Just looking at the cash inside the envelope, Armand can tell it is at least four thousand dollars. Armand replies," Yes this is probably more than enough."

"If you can find proof of my husband's infidelity, I will get you more" says Cheryll.

Armand, who finishes his cigarette replies, "Very well then. I will book myself a flight and reserve a hotel room. Once I find out something, I will set up a meeting with you and we will go over the evidence, if there is any."

"Thank you for your time and your help, Mr. Gerhart, I mean Armand", says Cheryl with a stoic but assured looks on her face."

"Don't thank me just yet. Let's wait and see if I find anything. Let me walk you out." says Armand.

Armand walks Cheryl out of the office and to the elevators. As he returns Armand says to Janine, his assistant," Janine, I will need you to book me a flight to Las Vegas, next Thursday and reserve a room at the Plaza."

Janine replies," Sure thing Armand. Another cheating spouse case?"

"Yes, how did you guess?" asks Armand. I have been here long enough to know what that sorrowful look on a person's face means," replies Janine.

"You are learning. You may just be a detective yet. In the meantime, I will let the rest of the staff know that I will be gone."

Armand walks back to his office. He stairs outside and enjoys the bustling view of traffic in downtown Chicago.

CHAPTER 2

As the sun sets over the city of Las Vegas on a November night, the dazzling lights of the Las Vegas strip become brighter and illuminate all of Sin City.

Armand had deboarded his plane and passes the baggage claim and steps outside. He smokes a cigarette quickly before hailing a taxi. "Where are you going sir?" asks the taxi driver. "The Plaza," answers Armand as he enters the taxi.

From the airport to the hotel riding in the taxi, Armand gazes outside to view the spectacular Las Vegas strip. But he is staying downtown which may be less grand but no less amusing and tempting.

Armand thinks to himself and wonders how Elena's trip will be in Austin as she leaves for the Texas capital tomorrow to provide catering to a tech convention.

But he also thinks about how he told her that he was going to San Diego instead of Las Vegas. Why indeed did he conceal his true whereabouts to his wife? Perhaps because Armand prefers to keep his cases and his clients a secret from everyone outside his office, even his own wife, Elena. Besides suppose Elena does know Kevin Price, her knowledge of Armand's investigation could jeopardize the case.

The taxi arrives at the Plaza Hotel. Armand pays the driver, grabs his luggage, and enters the casino and smells the lingering odor of cigarette smoke and alcohol. Beeping sounds and chimes of the slot machines can be heard. It is not super busy in the casino but still a descent crowd of exciting gamblers looking for that big jackpot.

As Armand marches through the casino towards the front lobby, booming cheering from a group of delighted gamblers at a blackjack table can be heard.

Entering the lobby, Armand opts to have a seat in the lobby area instead of approaching the front desk.

Armand reveals his laptop computer from his carry-on bag and turns it on. The skilled private investigator has a special hacking program on his computer that allows him access to guests staying at a hotel and what room they have been assigned.

This program is not only considered to be illegal but unethical as well. However, it proves to be a useful tool when tracking someone. To Armand it is a necessary evil and a means to an end.

Armand is able to hack into the guest database at the Plaza and searches for Kevin Price who has been assigned room 1901.

Kevin has not yet arrived, and the room below is vacant, which is excellent news for Armand as it will be easier to monitor Mr. Price.

Conspicuously, setting his laptop back into his bag, Armand walks briskly towards the front desk and is greeted by the attendant.

"Greetings sir, how can I help you?" asks the front desk attendant.

Armand hands his identification and credit card to the attendant along with a fifty-dollar bill and answers." I have a reservation under the name of Gerhart, Armand Gerhart."

"Yes Mr. Gerhart, it looks like we have a deluxe room available. However, I could upgrade you to a suite," the attendant replies as he slyly tucks the fifty-dollar bill in his pocket.

"That would be terrific. By chance is room 1801 in the north tower available. A friend of mine highly recommended it?" asks Armand in a gracious and cordial manor.

The attendant replies, "We sure do, and it is an excellent room." Typing in his computer the young and energetic front desk attendant confirms," Ok, Mr. Gerhart we have you in suite 1801 in the north tower. Check out is normally at eleven o'clock in the morning but I can give you a late check out at one o'clock in the afternoon. The elevators are to your right. Have a pleasant stay sir."

"Thank you. I am sure I will," responds Armand as he walks towards the elevators.

*****

Moments later, Armand walks into his large and wide-open room and drops his luggage on the king-size bed. He looks out the window and enjoys the splendid view of downtown Las Vegas. Armand grabs his laptop computer and sets it up on the ample desk.

Armand leaves his room and spots a housekeeping cart. Besides having towels and cleaning supplies on the cart there are also some room key cards, more than likely, master keys for housekeeping that can access any guest room.

Checking his surroundings cautiously, Armand doesn't see anyone around, so he takes one of the cards and enters the elevator and goes to the next floor.

As he steps off the elevator, Armand walks to the end of the hallway to room 1901, the room that is assigned to Kevin Price.

Armand uses the room key card he took from the cart and gains access to room 1901. He walks in and surveys the room for the best locations. Armand has some micro cameras that also provide audio that he can access from his computer.

These micro cameras are about half the size of a ballpoint pen. Armand finds a spot by the television and another by the ceiling light. Both locations are ideal as they cover most of the room and are inconspicuous.

*****

The next evening Armand is sitting steadily in his hotel room monitoring his computer intently. From his computer, Armand has been viewing Kevin's room.

So far Armand has observed Kevin entering the room but no other woman up to this point as Kevin hasn't spent much time in the room.

It is late this night, almost midnight and Armand has fallen asleep at the desk in his room. His head is lying on top of his crossed arms on the desk next to his computer.

Screams and moans of erotic passion wake Armand. He immediately lifts his head up and his wide awake as he observes the video footage from Kevin's room.

Kevin is with another woman. He has his back to the camera and the woman is bent over the bed. The woman is also turned away from the camera as Kevin is thrusting inside her from behind.

As the couple continue with their passionate encounter, the woman is heard screaming in the thrills of ecstasy, "Don't stop, don't stop I'm almost there!" Kevin begins smacking the woman on her ass as his erythematic forces get faster and faster.

"Come on you horny bitch. Turn around so I can see your face.," Armand says impatiently as he zooms on the two participants.

Just then Kevin tosses the woman on her back as he continues to penetrate her canal. The woman's face is now visible on the camera.

A feeling of shock and dread fills Armand. He cannot believe what he is witnessing. "This can't be. Am I really seeing this?" Armand says in total bewilderment and denial.

His jaw, if it weren't attached to his face, would fall to the floor. Feelings of sudden shock have turned to thoughts of deep betrayal. Rage begins to fill Armand like helium filling a balloon. A balloon that is ready to burst. A balloon of feelings and thoughts now bursts with obscenities from Armand's mouth as he slams his fist on the desk and yells," That goddamn treacherous slut!!!"

The slut Armand speaks of. The woman that is on camera is Armand's wife, Elena.

CHAPTER 3

It is the Saturday evening following Armand's disturbing discovery concerning the affair between Kevin Price and Armand's wife Elena.

Cheryl Price is sitting at a table and anxiously waiting in a lounge in an upscale hotel in downtown Saint Louis.

She looks around the lounge which overlooks the lobby area of the massive hotel. The lounge itself is faintly lit with the noise of about a dozen patrons talking in the background. There is also a man playing a relaxing and soothing song on a piano that is in the center of the lounge.

Cheryl is waiting for Armand to appear as he contacted her the previous night while he was still in Las Vegas. Armand had notified Cheryl that he had essential information regarding her husband, Kevin, and needed to meet with her in person.

Armand is seen by Cheryl walking towards the lounge. As she spots him, Cheryl waves at Armand to get his attention, who quickly notices Cheryl and makes his way towards her and says with a dour look on his," Hello, Mrs. Price."

Cheryl responds as she feels an upset feeling in her stomach, "It doesn't look like you have very good news."

"I'm afraid I don't," replies Armand who then asks," Can I get you a drink because I sure need one?"

"Please, a glass of red wine. Perhaps a cabernet?" answers Cheryl in a meek tone.

Armand walks leisurely to the bar and orders a glass of wine for Cheryl and a bourbon for him. He walks swiftly back to the table and hands Cheryl her drink as he sits down across from her.

Cheryl taking a sip of her wine and with a worried look on her face as her stomach tightens like a ball old twine asks," I take it by the look on your face, you have bad news?"

With a bitter and detached stare on his face as his heart has been ripped out of him, Armand answers," I am afraid so. Your husband has been having an affair but not with random women in each city but with one woman who has met him in each city."

Cheryl feels a swarm of emotion. She is somewhat relieved to finally know the truth as the suspicions of her husband's infidelity has been looming over her for so long, but she is also saddened and heartbroken after all Kevin and her have been together since they first met in high school. Though she is also enraged as the confirmation of her husband's betrayal sets in and she asks lividly, "Who is this bitch and how long has it been going on?"

Armand feels the same pain and torment as Cheryl as he has also been betrayed. He looks upon Cheryl with an empathetic look and answers," Based on what I witnessed on video and audio this has been going on since this past February. Going back to Atlanta then Houston, Indianapolis, Philadelphia and six other cities where Kevin and this woman could trace both of them in the same city and the same hotel."

Both eager and irritated to hear the whole truth, Cheryl with a few tears in her eyes asks once again," But who is this woman, this slut. I will rip her tits off."

Armand is somewhat surprised by Cheryl's anger as she has shown herself to be a such a soft and gentle soul. He is even now impressed by her rage. He expected to see her fall apart but instead Cheryl shows a strength in her.

Inhaling the rest of his bourbon, Armand looks at Cheryl with melancholy eyes and answers," The slut is my wife."

Cheryl gasps and covers her mouth with her hands and says," Oh my I'm so sorry" as both her and Armand share a brief awkward moment of silence. Cheryl asks, "Your wife, my husband, how can this be?"

Armand replies with a deep sigh," My wife, Elena owns and operates a catering service and apparently has a contract with your husband's conventions." Armand shakes his head still in disbelief and says," I can't believe she would do this to me or your husband to you."

"So now what?" asks Cheryl sternly and continues, "I suppose we have enough evidence to divorce both of them?"

"Yes, divorce them so they can be free to be together," replies Armand with malice in his voice.

"Doesn't seem fair. Sure, we could divorce them, but we would be just setting them free so those two can have their happily ever after," responds Cheryl with a sour look.

"It is like we would be doing them a favor when we should be getting some sort of retribution for what they have done to us," replies Armand in an agreeable tone.

As Armand and Cherly continue their discussion, little do they know that their conversation is being overheard by a woman sitting at a nearby table.

The woman listening to Armand and Cheryl is a vampire who is over four hundred years old named Lillith, who like many vampires has exceptional hearing and when she concentrates can hear any conversation within a nearby distance.

The experienced and cunning vampire has taken quite an interest in Armand and Cheryl's dilemma and believes she can be of some assistance to them both.

Lillith stands up and begins to walk confidently towards Armand and Cheryl. Both Armand and Cheryl take notice of Lillith, and both admire her long deep brown hair and her buxom figure as she is dressed in blue jeans and a low-cut black blouse.

Approaching their table, Lillith smiles and says, "Excuse me, pardon the interruption but I must confess I was eavesdropping, which is an awful habit of mine. May I sit down?"

Armand with a puzzled look on his face look over to Cheryl who shares Armand's perplexity and curiosity. Cheryl gives him a look saying with her facial expression, 'sure invite her.'

'Of course, "Have a seat my name is Armand, and this is my client, Cheryl and you are?" responds Armand.

As Lillith sits next to Armand and across Cheryl answers," My name is Lillith Tesio." Lillith looks over towards the bartender who immediately leaves his station and walk towards the table and asks," May I get you some more drinks, miss."

Lillith immediately responds," a round of drinks for the three of us; a bourbon for the gentleman, a glass of cabernet for the lovely redhead and another old fashioned for me."

The bartender nods and says, "coming right up folks." As he returns to the bar.

"Given your accent and name, I take it you are from Italy or at least Italian descent?" Armand asks.

Lillith responds with a devious smile," I was born and raised in Milan. But have lived in several other countries; Romania, France, Germany, Scotland and here in the States."

The bartender brings the drinks to the table and hands the drinks to each of the trio of possible collaborators.

"Just charge those drinks to my room please.," requests Lillith. The bartender replies with a smile, "Of course" and walks back towards the bar.

Armand is thinking,' What does this woman want with us. Yes, she is very sexy but that is not always a trustworthy attribute.' Cheryl is thinking similarly to Kevin and with a suspenseful look on her face.

Lillith, with a grin," I am aware of your mutual heartache and your dilemma, and I think I can be of service to both of you."

Armand who is intrigued by Lillith asks," How can you help us?"

"Yes, with all due respect. You eavesdrop on our conversation, then interrupt us and think you can squirm your way with us by buying us drinks," says Cheryl who has become irritable and annoyed.

Cheryl regains her composure and feels embarrassed for lashing out like she did and says in a calmer manor," Please forgive me. That was rude. It is just exceedingly difficult right now."

Lillith gives a reassuring look towards Cheryl and reaches for her hand and holds it gently and says," Don't apologize. I do tend to be a bit forward at times. I understand this is a traumatic time for both of you. You have both had your hearts ripped out of your chests like discarded broken parts in a car."

"You have a gift for reading people. I will give you that, but what can you do for us?" asks Armand.

"I can help you both get closure and most importantly revenge" says Lillith with a gleam in her eye." Furthermore, you will both be helping me in the process."

Both Armand and Cheryl look at each other and Armand turns to Lillith and states," Ok, lets here what you have to say."

Lillith responds," I have a proposition. A proposition that will be mutually beneficial to all three of us. Tell me, have either of you been to Scotland? Furthermore, what do you know of." Lillith pauses and smiles as she looks at both Armand and Cheryl and then says in a cryptic manor, "Vampires."

TALE 4: THE VASILE ORDER

CHAPTER 1

It is the early 1600's, in the Romanian town of Medias which is located in the province of Transylvania. A territory full of folklore from ravaging werewolves to blood thirsty vampires.

Warm weather is felt throughout the small town as spring transitions to summer. The pleasant fragrance of blossoming flowers infiltrate the air in the town. A welcomed transition from the rancid odor of corpses taken by leprosy or war. Much of the population of the working-class town has been decimated due to plagues of leprosy and The Fifteen Year War which engulfed all of Romania.

The sun has set, and the moon has risen as darkness falls on Medias on this pleasantly warm but humid evening.

A married couple argues in a cozy cottage within the city. The husband, a local merchant by the name of Alin Albu, a hefty bearded and unpleasant man yells at his insolent wife.

"You stupid wench. You call this dinner." Alin yells at his wife as he throws the bowl of soup across the kitchen area of their two-room cottage, which is made of stone throughout.

Alin's wife, Mariana whose surname is Bacur has been married to Alin less than a month. A marriage that was arranged by their parents which is the only explanation why a strikingly beautiful woman with Greek goddess features from her long black hair, curvy figure and captivating brown eyes would have anything to do with a revolting and abrasive slob like Alin.

"You loathsome pig. You wouldn't know tasty food if someone dumped it on your fat head," yells Mariana, who is not the type of woman to take any abuse towards her flippantly. An attribute not very well celebrated in her community and culture which demands a woman to be subservient to her husband.

Mariana proceeds to dump a bowl of soup right on Alin's head which scalds her abusive husband. "There you can eat it or wear it," as Mariana mocks Alin and begins to chuckle.

In pain from the burning sensation from the top of his head throughout his face, Alin shouts" You bitch, I should cut you into a thousand pieces."

Alin strikes a viscous blow towards Mariana on the left side of her face with the back of his right hand.

Mariana falls backwards and collapses to the floor but where most women would cry and cower, Mariana stands up defiantly and throws a meat clever at Alin which barely misses his head. Full of rage, Alin grabs Mariana by the throat, kicks open the door to the cottage and throws Mariana out the cottage like a rag doll.

Alin still screaming in pain yells," Get out of my fucking house you cunt until you learn some fucking manners. I should tell your parents about your insolence. They will disown you and you can live the rest of your life as a penniless whore."

"Tell them what you will. I give no shits of their thoughts of me. And by the way I gain no pleasure whenever you stick that cock of yours in me. In fact, I wish to vomit every time, "screams back, Mariana in boldness and fury.

"Fuck off bitch", shouts Alin as he slams the cottage door shut in a booming and forceful sound that several people nearby can hear like a crack of thunder.

The deafening commotion is heard by a local Transylvanian nobleman dressed in all black except for the burgundy red lining of his cape and the satin red vest.

The nobleman is Count Bogdan Vasile of the House Vasile which lies on the outskirts of Medias. He thinks, 'That is no way to treat a lovely woman like that and perhaps I should gut the useless excuse of a human. Or maybe this woman doesn't necessarily need a savior but a teacher. Someone to show her how to fight for herself.'

Mariana is now sitting in the middle of the road wearing a grey dress with a white chemise underneath. She looks up at the sky which is full of stars and sheds a few tears, not for being physically manhandled or even having her feelings hurt. No, she sheds those tears to the pure horror and dread which is her life. 'Is this what marriage really is? Is this what love is supposed to be? Is the rest of my life doomed with misery,' the thoughtful young woman asks herself in silence.

Looking towards the ever-ending row of cottages stacked one after another like rows of cattle, Mariana notices a stranger walking towards her.

The stranger is Bogdan, who looks down on Mariana who is still sitting on the pavement and is looking back up at Bogdan.

"It looks like you have had a bit of an accident my lady may I help you to your feet, "asks Bogdan as he offers his assistance to Mariana by offering his hand. He was already impressed her spirit and fight but is now mesmerized by her striking beauty as he stares at her brown eyes and her face which may be bruised on one side but even that bruise cannot hide Mariana's smooth and stunning facial features.

"Of course, and thank you", replies Mariana as she takes Bogdan's hand who helps Mariana to her feet.

As Mariana brushes the dirt and dust off her dress she stares at Bogdan's face and is just as enamored with Bogdan's handsome features as Bogdan is with her gorgeous demeanor. She is captivated by Bogdan's eyes which are as big and brown as hers.

"Let me permit me to introduce myself. I am Count Vasile, Bogdan Vasile", greets the noble count.

"I have heard of you my Count your charitable contributions have been quite a welcome to this community. I am Mariana Bacur or at least I used to be my married name is Albu," replies Mariana.

"So, am I to surmise, that was your husband who so disgustingly tossed you out on to this street?" asks Bogdan.

"Unfortunately, that walking filthy pile of shit is my husband", answers Mariana who is ashamed of this moment.

"I loathe bad manners from those of such low disposition. I have a good mind to rip his head off and drink blood from his empty skull," states Bogdan in a serious tone.

As grotesque as Bogdan's statement may have been. Mariana smiles and even laughs. She replies," Well you wouldn't have to spend too much time hallowing out his head as his brain can't be any bigger than the size of a pebble."

"Perhaps I shall show you how to do such a thing to such a walking waste of filth," Bogdan says with a sinful smile and continues to asks," "Why would you get married to such a ridiculous buffoon. Surely, a woman of your beauty and intellect could find a much more appropriate suitor?"

"Well, I didn't have much of a choice. It was an arranged marriage between his parents and mine," answers Mariana with regret.

"You deserve much better," replies Bogdan and continues to say," There is an inviting little tavern down the road from here. May I interest you in something to eat or even some wine?"

"I don't have much of an appetite but could use something to drink," answers Mariana who then asks. "But what if people see us together?"

Bogdan answers with a reassuring smile," You don't strike me as a woman who cares too much what other people think. Besides where we are going no one is going to say much. After all I own the place."

Mariana smiles back and says, "Then take me to your tavern, dear sir."

*****

Several minutes later, Mariana and Bogdan are sitting down at a table in the corner of the quaint and resting tavern.

There are several local towns people eating, drinking, and socializing as it is a Saturday evening, a good time to celebrate the spoils of a sustained week of labor.

Mariana and Bogdan are sharing a bottle of wine and eating off a tray of cheese and slices of meat as Mariana has regained her appetite.

Mariana asks Bogdan," Be honest Count, how bad is the bruise on my face."

Bogdan takes a sip of wine and observes Mariana's face and answers," It's not good but I have seen worse."

"I suppose you have seen worse. I have heard you fought in the Fifteen Year War under Giorgio Basta. I even heard you were the one who killed Michael the Brave?" Mariana pauses thinking she might be talking too much as her parents always scolded her for talking out of turn as does her husband, Alin. She continues," I apologize. I am probably being too intrusive."

"There is nothing to apologize about. I did fight in the war, and I was the one who killed Michael the Brave," answers Bogdan who shakes his head while smiling and says, "Michael the Brave? There was nothing brave about that arrogant tyrant. He received what he deserved."

Bogdan looks over towards Mariana and says," If you don't mind me saying, you are a beautiful lady and you have quite the spirit. I admire that in a woman."

Blushing, Mariana replies, "Thank you my Count and you are quite the gentleman yourself; handsome and intelligent. I wish I had met you over a month ago. Perhaps I could have avoided this travesty of a marriage that I am trapped in."

"Who says, you have to remain imprisoned in a miserable marriage that was against your will. You could leave that the sloth, "responds Bogdan.

"Are you not aware of the ways of the world or have you spent too much time in that ancient home of yours?" asks Mariana who also says," As a young woman I have no say in my life."

"I am fully aware of the ways of mortals but in my world, it wouldn't have to be that way. In my world we can make our own rules and determine our own destiny," replies Bogdan.

Mariana is somewhat mystified and curious about Bogdan's answer. She is well aware of rumors that has spread throughout Medias that Count Bogdan Vasile is a vampire, an undead creature who sleeps during the day and roams the night to feed on the living. Mariana always thought all those rumors were mere nonsense.

Mariana replies with surprise in her voice to Bogdan," Your world? Your world is the same as ours. Unless the speculations and gossip is true about you."

"And what speculations might those be?" asks Bogdan who has an assured smile on his face.

Somberly, Mariana answers, "That my dear Count, you are a vampire, much like the legendary Prince Vlad Teppes was rumored to be."

"I see you are well versed in Romanian and Transylvanian history and folklore. I am impressed. You truly are as clever as you are radiant," responds Bogdan.

"Flattery will only get you so far Count Vasile," Mariana says with a smirk. "I am not sure if I believe in all of those stories of vampires and werewolves."

"What if I told you that vampires were real and that I am indeed a vampire?" Bogdan asks.

Mariana replies sarcastically," I would say prove it. Of course, without sucking my blood. I know I have a cross which vampires are supposed to be repelled by."

Mariana has a cross around her neck and takes it off and holds it up to Bogdan's face who sits back in his chair and yawns as the cross in Mariana's hand begins to heat up like a piece of meat roasting over an open fire.

Mariana immediately drops the cross on the table and holds her hand which was burning but the pain has gone away as quickly as it developed.

She looks up at Bogdan and thinks, 'What just happened? Did he do that?'

"Sorry about that," says Bogdan, "I hope that didn't hurt too much", as he holds the hand that was burnt from Mariana.

"It's fine now. What kind of trick was that? Are you some kind of wizard or magician?" Mariana asks as she pulls her hand away from Bogdan.

"I told you I am a vampire. Crosses have no effect on us despite what folklore would have you believe. Though it is true we don't do so well in the daylight, and we don't reflect in mirrors," replies Bogdan.

If Bogdan really is a vampire, Mariana should be scared but instead she is genuine in her curiosity and is now even more attracted to Bogdan.

"What about garlic?" asks Mariana. Bogdan laughs and replies, "Garlic, such nonsense. I remember about twenty years ago a man and a woman who were vampire slayers were going to try to kill me and they were both wearing garlic around their necks. I ended up bending both of them over and shoved my cock in both their asses while I was sucking them dry."

Mariana is at first stunned but then giggles while stating, "So you take with men as well as women?"

Bogdan answers, "Vampires will take with anyone we desire to take with, though I do prefer females. But in that case, it was more about humiliating them then it was about any sexual desire. I hope that doesn't scare you."

"I suppose it should, but it doesn't" replies Mariana and gleefully says," I suppose if I had a cock, I would shove it up my husband's fat hairy ass."

Both Bogdan and Mariana laugh. Mariana asks, "So Count Bogdan Vasile. Just how old are you and how many women have you defiled?"

"I am a hundred and fifteen years old and I estimate about a hundred and seven women, some of whom I turned into vampires", Bogdan answers and asks," Just why are so interested in my exploits?"

"Just curious, that's mighty impressive", answers Mariana and then asks," So do all these women you have turned into vampires live with you in your home?"

"They have in the past, but most have gone exploring the world. Right now, it's just me and me loyal servant and ghoul, Nicholas, who watches over my humble home," answers Bogdan.

Bogdan looks straight into Mariana's eyes and asks," tell me, you don't seem to be the least scared that I am a Vampire. You, also, don't seem to be disgusted by the amount of women I have been with. Why?"

"Perhaps, I am not satisfied that you are a vampire. Perhaps I am just enjoying the conversation which is far more tantalizing than any words spoken by my husband. As far as your exploits, why as beings should we be limited to just one love the rest of our lives. Don't get me wrong I would love to have a man to worship as long as he worshiped me back. Unfortunately, fate and life has not given me that," responds eloquently, Mariana.

Bogdan is impressed by Mariana's words as well has her confidence and boldness. He senses a strength in Mariana that is equal to her beauty. Bogdan, who wants not just a bride but an equal, a queen to his king and countess to his count.

"You are wrong about fate my dear. I can change your fate and importantly your destiny. I can show you how to avenge the dishonor that was laid to you by your husband but even more importantly than that, I can give you eternal life as well as bliss," responds Bogdan who also says," Just come back with me to my quaint yet hospitable home."

Intrigued and enticed by Bogdan's offer, Mariana, who is very much attracted to Bogdan in a way, has never been before with anyone. Only her teenage love could come close. She thinks to herself,' Is this count really a vampire and if so, does he mean to turn me into his bride? All the nonsense I have had to endure between my doting parents and their oppressive religious beliefs which have led me to be married to a vile sloth of a human being.'

"Sure, why not? Even if you drain my blood dry. It couldn't be any worse than what awaits for me should I return to my home," answers Mariana.

Bogdan stands up and grabs Mariana's hand the one that was burnt. He kisses her hand and says," Then follow me my lady and I will show you true pleasure."

*****

Bogdan is giving Mariana a tour of his quaint castle like home. It is not a large castle as it is only two stories but made entirely of Greystone. The downstairs has three large rooms: a dining room, a kitchen, and a study. While the upstairs has three bedrooms. A cellar lies beneath the foundation where a row of coffins are present.

Bogdan and Mariana are in the study area where a large bookcase takes up an entire wall. There is also a fireplace but as this is a warm and sultry night there is no need for the fire to burn.

Nicholas, Bogdan's servant, and ghoul, which is a creature turned by a vampire that often feeds on the blood of insects. Like a vampire a ghoul is ageless but unlike a vampire, they can absorb the sunlight thus making them protectors and caretakers as their vampire masters sleep during the day, pours some wine into a glass for Mariana and then takes his leave has he has been dismissed by Bogdan.

"Thank you for your assistance, Nicholas. We shall see you tomorrow evening,' states Bogdan.

"We? I believe you assume to much my count," announces Mariana with a grin.

Bogdan responds," I do not believe you are in such a hurry to retire to your home. I would think I am much better company."

"Oh, you are for sure," replies Mariana as she sips the last of her wine as she is sitting on a red velvet couch." So, tell me my count, are there strict rules when being a vampire?"

Bogdan who is standing sits down next to Mariana and says," There are the basic rules. We cannot be in the sunlight, that is our biggest curse along with we are unable to bear children, which given the harsh brutality of the world may be a blessing instead of a curse."

The count continues," However once a being is fully initiated as a vampire, they will never age another day and will become stronger. I myself have the strength and reflexes of many men and have the ability to shape myself into a bat or even a wolf. We can only be destroyed by sunlight, a steak driven through our hearts or decapitation."

Mariana asks," Vampires also feed on the blood of the living, don't they? I suppose you would feed on anyone?"

"All vampires have their own codes", replies Bogdan." Some will feed on anyone or anything but there are some of us who are more selective. I typically only target those mortals who are of questionable character and in this world, there is no shortage of those type of souls."

"Not to get too sentimental but are vampires capable of love and if so, have you been in love?" asks Mariana.

"There has been evidence of such things happening to vampires. In fact, it was a loving and blissful couple who initiated me. Initiates means to fully turn a mortal to a vampire. We call it the initiation of blood. As far as myself is considered I have yet to know that feeling of love. At least not yet," Bogdan answers and then asks," What about you have you been in love or at least laid with another man besides your husband?"

Mariana, remembering her past love as a teenager, replies," There was a young man named Juri. When I was seventeen years of age. He was of the same age and was a farm boy on the outskirts of town. I wanted to be with him more than anything."

"What happened to him? Why didn't you marry him?" asks Bogdan.

Mariana sighs and a melancholy look appears on her face. She answers," My parents wouldn't allow it. They were dead set on marrying me off to Alin as they were good friends with his parents."

Bogdan feels the sadness in Mariana and feels empathy towards her as he never has for any mortal, at least not since he became a vampire.

Mariana also, says," I told my parents that I wanted to marry Juri and that I would run off with him. They scoffed at me and told me it wasn't my decision to make. One evening Juri's dead corpse was found floating in the lake, his throat had been slit and his body dumped in the lake."

Standing up and turning away from Bogdan, Mariana begins to cry and says," Someone murdered him and whether it was my parents, Alin's parents or Alin himself.

Bogdan slowly rises to his feet and gradually walks towards Mariana. He hands her a handkerchief to dry her weeping eyes.

Mariana takes the handkerchief and caresses her eyes and tears fall like a steady rain.

Bogdan stands behind her and places his hands on Mariana's shoulders and says in an easy voice," You must not blame or otherwise torture yourself over Juri's death my lady. I cannot promise that I can take away all your pain, but I can promise you I will treat you like a queen from this day forward."

"You wish me to be your countess? Do you wish to initiate me? Why?" asks Mariana who is puzzled but then looks at a full mirror in front of her and notices that Bogdan throws no reflection.

"Oh my, I cannot see you in this mirror. "You are a vampire!" Mariana says as her cynicism towards Bogdan's true identity becomes a comforted reality. Mariana is almost pleased that Bogdan is a vampire after all.

"I am as I told you before. Now follow me to my chambers and I will provide you answers to your questions", replies Bogdan.

Mariana follows Bogdan up the spiral staircase. As they both reach the landing of the second floor, Bogdan grabs a lit torch which was mounted on the wall and Mariana follows him down the dark secluded hallway.

They both come to a door and using his telepathic powers, Bogdan opens the door and Bogdan and Mariana enter the room. Bogdan lights a few more torches to provide some light as the room's only window is covered by large black drapes that are black as night. The aroma of sulfur from the torches fill the air in the room.

Mariana notices a large bed that could easily fit four, maybe even five grown adults comfortably. The bedding is burgundy red with the headboard being black. She also notices two coffins lying on the floor at the foot of the bed.

Bogdan turns towards Mariana and gazes into her eyes, He would normally use his hypnotic powers on Mariana but has chosen to let her use her own freewill.

Answering Mariana's earlier questions Bogdan responds," Yes, I wish to initiate you as my bride and my countess. If that is your wish. As to why I have chosen you, I have been with many women over this past century some of whom I initiated. But none were worthy of my full devotion. You my dear Mariana have a strength, a loyalty and intelligence that I have not seen in a woman or man for that matter in a long time. I feel a love for you that I have never felt for any woman."

Mariana feels her heart beating faster and faster and she is captivated by Bogdan's words and his soul if a vampire has such a thing. She so wants to be with him.

Mariana feeling a lust and love she thought she could never feel again asks in a gleeful tone," What does this initiation entail my count?"

"I will drink your blood from your sultry neck then you will drink my blood. Then we will act on our lust for one another. During this process you will feel ecstasy and power you could not even imagine. Then you will be my loving countess," Bogdan says with a calm but alluring tone.

Excitement and arousal consumes Mariana's body. Mariana says to Bogdan, "It would be my pleasure to be your countess and to be your bride of love and blood."

With those words Mariana passionately kisses Bogdan who reciprocates the kiss. They both tear each other's clothes off.

Bogdan caresses and kisses on Mariana's exposed breasts as Mariana begins stroking Bogdan's cock.

Grabbing Mariana with passion, Bogdan holds her naked body up against his. Fangs begin to emerge from his mouth as his dick goes from semi flaccid to fully erect. Mariana can feel Bogdan's shaft rubbing up against her pussy which is getting damp.

Bogdan eyes become red and opens his mouth wider than even a wolf and with one swift motion bites into Mariana's bare neck and begins sucking her blood.

Mariana feels a warmth in her, she could only imagine in her dreams but now those dreams are becoming a reality as the more Bogdan bites into her, the closer she gets to orgasmic bliss.

Bogdan throws Mariana to the bed, and she lands on her back as he reveals a dagger which he uses to instantly slice his wrist.

The site of Bogdan's blood provokes Mariana as much as Bogdan's physique. She sits back up and throws her mouth towards Bogdan's wrist and begins slurping up his blood.

Mariana's eyes go from brown to yellow and then to blood red, The whole room as well as Bogdan turn a shade of crimson.

Sexual phrenzy spreads throughout both Mariana and Bogdan. Mariana feels aggressive, grabs Bogdan, and throws him to the bed on his back.

Mariana climbs on Bogdon's cock like a rider jumping on a horse and begins slowly throttling his cock with her pussy.

A slow steady pace becomes faster and faster as fangs appear from Mariana's mouth and Bogdan pulls himself up towards Mariana as the two lock each other's tongues together with their open mouths.

Simultaneously they each bite into each other's necks as these two gothic lovers become one and Mariana cums as she screams at the top of her lungs.

Bogdan now the aggressor throws Mariana on her stomach and lifts her ass up in the air as he penetrates her from behind.

Thrusting faster and harder for several minutes. Mariana has another intense orgasm as Bogdan's cock erupts inside her with a gush of cum.

The vampire count and his new countess lie in bed side by side catching their breath as their fangs retreat into their mouths and their eyes regain their original big brown color.

As they both look into each other's eyes and smile gleefully, Mariana asks with a confident smirk," I suppose this means my previous marriage has been annulled?"

"You are quite right my love. You are now Countess Mariana Vasile, the matriarch of the Vasile order", answers Bogdan who returns the cocky smirk.

"I adore the sound of that title but not to damper our moods, what should be done with that pig of a former husband of mine?" Mariana asks.

"The remainder of the night belongs to us my lovely countess. Before the sun rises, we will adjourn to our coffins. When the sun sets tomorrow, we will pay the vile of vomit a visit and you will teach him some manners," responds Bogdan.

"Then my handsome count I look forward to your teachings in this matter," Mariana responds with excitement as the two vampires embrace each other; flesh on flesh, blood for blood and soul to soul.

*****

The next evening Alin is sitting alone in his house. He is eating some bread and drinking wine.

Earlier that day he had told his parents along with Mariana's parents of the argument he had with Mariana the night before,

He was chastised like a schoolboy by both his parents and Mariana's for throwing her out and letting her wander off.

They had spent all day searching for his lost wife and even reported her missing to the local authorities.

It has become gusty outside as a summer storm moves into the town of Meridia. The wind begins whistling outside and Alin stands up to close the shudders to the windows as the wind is blowing rain mist inside the cottage.

As he looks around his empty home, which smells like a stable as the odor of the horses and the donkey that sit outside out back of the cottage lingers inside, Alin wonders if Mariana will return.

He is less concerned about his wife than his or her parents, but he does consider Mariana to be his property and wants her back to serve his every needs.

It has begun raining outside and the sounds of pitter patter can be heard as the rain pelts the ground and Alin can smell the pungent whiff of rain.

Without warning the howling wind immediately blows open one of sets of shudders inside Alin's home and rains begins blowing in.

"Ah fuck" yells Alin as he goes to close the shudders. Yet as he closes the wooden shudders, they blow back open and hit him in his face causing his lip to bleed.

As blood drips from his lower lip Alin roars, "Shit, shit, damnit" as he grips a piece of cloth and applies pressure to the fresh wound.

A light faint tapping sound is heard from the front door.

"Who the hell could that be?," says an annoyed and upset Alin as he walks towards the door.

Walking towards the door, Aiden growls in a burley voice "Who is it?" Alin opens the door and sees no one is there. He looks around outside as rain continues to pour down like a heavy shower. Alin yells out, "Whoever is out there, if you are looking for shelter, you will get none here." Alin then slams the door shut.

As he turns around, he is startled. Standing there across the dingy room is Mariana who is wearing a white evening gown that is low-cut and shows off her busty cleavage. Her long silky black hair is blowing from the wind that has blustered in the house. Her milky white skin is practically glowing in the dim home with only a few candles to provide any light. She is also wearing a black pendant around her neck with a red ruby at its center which was a gift from Bogdan.

"Is that anyway to greet your former wife," Mariana says in a scolding manner.

Mystified and in awe, Alin asks, "Where the fuck have you been you wench and what do you mean former wife? You can't divorce me."

"Oh, I am so sorry, but I have decided to improve my status and have taken a new husband", Mariana responds as she holds up her right hand that reveals a ring that matches the pendant around her neck.

Simultaneously Alin is both aroused by Mariana's beautiful and gothic appearance but is also enraged by her news. "How dare you bitch! It is not your place to leave me. I will have you burned like a witch," growls Alin.

"Oh, you poor thing," says Mariana as she mocks Alin and walks towards him. "I tell you what for old times' sake I will make it up to you this one time.

As she stands in front of Alin who is for once speechless as he is mesmerized by Mariana's eyes, she notices blood dripping from Alin's lower lip, and the site of his blood entices her as her beautiful brown eyes turn to a demonic red color.

Mariana goes to kiss Alin, who seizes the opportunity to grab Mariana and pull her closer to him. However, the bliss of the kiss turns horrifying as Mariana digs her teeth in his lower lip like a shark biting into its prey.

With one rapid motion, Mariana rips Alin's lower lip off with her teeth. Her fangs are fully exposed and Alin's blood dripping from her mouth. Mariana hisses at her former husband.

Alin, who is crying like a newborn infant drops to his knees grasping his open wound with blood gushing like a waterfall. Mariana states loudly towards outside," Ok, my love you may enter."

Bogdan enters the home dressed in a long black tailcoat with a white buttoned-down shirt wearing an identical pendant around his neck and a ring on his left ring finger which is similar to Mariana's. He is wearing a black top hat which he gently removes from his head and says to Alin in a welcoming voice, "Please to make your acquaintance."

"Oh, where are my manners," says Mariana. Alin this is my new husband; Count Bogdan Vasile and I am now Countess Mariana Vasile."

Mariana crouches down in front of Alin who is still weeping in pain and says in a scolding manner, "You disgusting piece of pig shit. It is about time someone taught you a lesson in manners."

With those words with one severe striking motion, Mariana penetrates Alin's chest with her hand and with one sudden motion rips Alin's heart out of his chest.

The heart is still beating but ever slowly as Alin looks on in shock and terror. Alin witnesses Mariana taking a bite out of his heart like it was an apple. With one last breath, Alin gasps and falls over dead.

"Mimicking a surprised look on her face, Mariana turns around and looks upward towards her new love and says elatedly," My loving count, dinner is served."

CHAPTER 2

It is springtime in Milan, Italy almost a decade after the fateful first encounter of Bogdan and Mariana.

It is a warm Sunday evening as the sun sets and the moon rises as there are no clouds in the sky. Only stars are seen in the dark sky twinkling. It is like the souls that reside in the heavens are blinking their eyes at those wandering the earth below.

Count Bogdan Vasile and Countess Mariana Vasile are seen walking the streets of Milan. Gradually walking arm and arm they marvel at the architecture of each building which stand next to one another.

Mariana is wearing a long crimson red low cut evening dress whose sleeves cover her whole arms. While Bogdan is wearing his usual long black coat, pants that match the darkness of his coat and his slicked black hair.

He is also wearing a white buttoned shirt underneath a burgundy vest.

Bogdan asks Mariana," So my countess how are you enjoying your first time in Italy?"

Amazed by the sounds and sights of the streets of Milan, Mariana responds," Oh its quite lovely and the views are breathtaking. Not to mention the food and wine are excellent far better than our home in Romania."

Mariana asks, "So how long has it been since you were last here, my count?"

"Let's see about forty-two years, I believe. I had also visited Venice and Naples on that trip", Bogdan answers.

"Venice was nice as well. Pity we will not make it to Naples on this trip," responds Mariana.

The count and countess hear an eruption of yelling down the street in which they are having a stroll. They walk over towards the commotion and find a small crowd of local townspeople gathering by the local church.

Standing in front of the entrance is a Catholic priest and the local magistrate. They motion the crowd of about eight people to silence themselves as they too are perplexed by the agitated crowd.

The magistrate dressed in gold armer asks the crowd, "Why all this commotion on this glorious sabbath evening?"

The people who are holding a young teenage girl push the girl to the ground at the feet of the magistrate and the priest. One of the men in the crowd asserts himself and says," This temptress seduced my son into sexual acts."

A woman in the crowd also says," She also seduced my impressionable daughter in those same lewd acts. It is a sin!"

The man whose son was seduced adds, "This young wench is a practitioner of Love Magic. It is the only explanation how she could have seduced our God-fearing children."

The magistrate asks," Well your children are of the same age, are they not?"

The mother of the girl seduced answers," They are but this temptress was caught by her own parents having relations with both my daughter and his son."

"This goes against scripture and is truly sinful," the priest says and then asks," Who is this girl's parents and what is her name?"

The father and mother of the temptress walk towards the front of the crowd and the father states," My name is Sergio, and this is my wife, Maria. We are Lillith's parents."

Maria," We believe she has the devil in her and must be exorcised."

The magistrate looks down on Lillith and commands, "Stand up Lillith. Do you have any words in your defense?"

Lillith, who is of slender build and long brown hair wearing an old brown torn garment that barely covers her, stands up sobbing and pleads, "I am not a devil nor am I possessed. We were just having some fun. They wanted to as well."

"You wicked bitch," says Lillith's mother," We raised you better than that."

Lillith who is still crying begs," Please papa, please mama don't send me away."

Sergio looks at Lillith with bitter scorn and replies in a cold voice, "You are no daughter of ours."

Lillith falls to her knees like a ton of bricks sobbing uncontrollably.

The magistrate motions with his right hand and two guards emerge from the shadows, grab Lillith, and take her away, as Lillith screams at the top of her lungs, "No, no, no."

From a distance Bogdan and Mariana observe the commotion. Mariana looks on towards Lillith with empathy and sadness as Lillith reminds Mariana of herself when she was her age.

"We will hold her overnight in the jail. "Now go back to your homes," announces the magistrate.

The priest tells the crowd," I will escort her to Rome tomorrow morning where she will be subject to inquisition. Our esteemed holy father, the Pope will decide her fate."

The bitter crowd shows their obedience and disburses back to their homes. The priest walks back into the church as the magistrate makes his way to the jail.

Bogdan looks towards Mariana and asks, "So you wish to rescue the young lady? "Mariana replies," Are you able to read my mind as well, I suppose."

"No, but I can read your face and expressions. She reminds you of you when you were younger?" replies and asks Bogdan.

"She does a little bit, but I would have spat at those old fools," Mariana says with contempt in her voice. "We could take her with us and raise her as our own."

"Raise a mortal?" Bogdan asks.

"We could initiate her when she is of age," Mariana replies.

"I see you have given this much thought," responds Bogdan, who pauses while in deep thought and says," I suppose it would be nice to have her with us. Should she choose to do so."

Bogdan looks back at Mariana who smiles with approval and with admiration for her count.

*****

About an hour later, Lillith is sitting in a cold, dark and damp jail cell, which is made of brick and mortar. The drab cell has one wooden door that is locked from the other side but there is one window that allows just enough fresh air into the cell but has three vertical metal bars designed to prevent escape.

Standing up, Lillith walks towards the window as if some kind of ominous force is pulling her in that direction.

A light cool breeze hits Lillith's dour face which is a welcome sensation. She is startled as a bat flies in between the bars of the window.

Lillith who has calmed her nerves as the bat does not frighten her. In fact, she sees a certain beauty in watching the bat flying about.

Flying around the cell the bat comes to a stop in the middle of the air and slowly transforms into a human female form.

Mariana emerges in front of Lillith who is in shock and disbelief at having witnessed such a sight. As she is stunned by the sight of witnessing a bat transform into a human. She is equally enamored with Mariana's regal exquisiteness. Lillith is a young woman who is equally attracted to women as she is men perhaps more so. Dressed in her red gown, Mariana appears to be a queen in the astonished eyes of Lillith.

"By the startled look on your face, it would seem you are due an explanation", Mariana says to Lillith in a confident and assuring manner.

"Excuse me for asking but I have heard stories and fables of vampires having the ability to transform into bats, but I never thought it was true. Are you a vampire my lady," asks Lillith.

"Those stories are true and yes I am a vampire", replies Mariana and then asks Lilith, "What is your name, young lady?"

Lillith replies," My name is Lillith Tesio, and I am sixteen years of age." Lillith often shows little to no respect for older adults as most adults in her life have judged her and demeaned her as Lillith would deny the teaching of scriptures and in the way she embraces her sexuality. But with Mariana whose beauty and elegance she admires, sees a woman she can learn from and respect as an elder.

"My name is Countess Mariana Vasile of the Romanian province of Transylvania," Mariana says as she walks slowly towards Lillith while observing every inch of Lillith. Mariana, who is just a bit taller than her younger acquaintance, stands almost eye to eye with Lillith as Mariana's brown eyes gazed into Lillith's hazel-colored eyes.

"Sixteen? You are quite developed for your age," says Mariana who begins to stride behind Lillith "My husband and I heard the commotion by the church earlier this evening. It would seem you have angered quite a few people including your parents."

Lillith, who is nervous as she is worried that Mariana will judge her, and she is equally worried about the guards who must standing close by.

A heavy mist seeps under the cell door like a heavy smoke. Lillith is bewildered by what appears to be fog. The heavy mist then compacts into a smaller form and soon the mist begins to convert into a male human form. As the mist disappears emerging from the fog is Bogdan.

Mystified, Lillith thinks she is losing her mind. First, she sees a bat turn into a woman and now, she sees mist turn into a man.

"Well, the guards won't be a problem," says Bogdan as he looks towards Mariana and then to Lillith.

"You didn't kill them, did you?" asks Mariana. "No, they seemed like descent men. Which is more than I can say for that flabby priest at the church," replies Bogdan who holds up a chalice filled with blood.

As Mariana takes the chalice from Bogdan she says," Oh where is my manners, Lillith this is my husband Count Bogdan Vasile. My husband this is Lillith," who takes a drink from the chalice.

"Please to meet you, young lady. Looks like you caused quite the stir earlier in the evening," as Bogdan introduces himself to Lillith who is almost as attracted to the tall handsome vampire as she is to Mariana.

Lillith genuflects towards Bogdan and says," It is my pleasure to meet you as well my count." As she stands up Lillith states," As I was about to tell your lovely wife, the countess, the reason I am being held in prison. It is because two friends of mine, Antone and Melissa were playing in a barn and well," Lillith pauses, and she begins to feel shame.

"Go on, you can tell us," urges Mariana. Bogdan adds, "Yes I've been roaming this earth over a hundred years and nothing you could say would surprise me."

Regaining her courage, Lillith says, "We are all of the same age, and we were just exploring ourselves. All of us consented after all I have heard stories in ancient Rome where this was a normal thing that was not frowned upon. Anyway, my parents caught us. Then all of the parents dragged me to the church."

"Why not condemn your friends as well, "asks Bogdan looking puzzled.

Lillith replies, "Because all of the adults in our neighborhood think I am some evil temptress because I refuse to adhere to the rules of the church, even my own parents think this. My parents think I used some sort of 'Love Magic' to seduce my friends."

Shaking her head in disgust Mariana says, "Typical, mortals so foolish in their beliefs."

"Is it any wonder Rome fell after they turned from their old gods and established the Catholic Church," responds Bogdan as Mariana hands him the chalice which he empties into his mouth.

"Are the two of you planning on feeding on me?" asks Lillith.

"Of course, not" replies Bogdan. "We wish to take you with us back to our home in Medias which is in Transylvania."

"You see as vampires we are unable to have children of our own so it would be nice to have you as our daughter. You could help our ghoul, Nicholas, with daily chores, but you will be free to live your life as you please with no judgement," adds Mariana.

"When the day comes and we feel you are mature enough, you will be given the choice to truly become one of us, a vampire in the Order of Vasile or if you wish to leave on your own, you can. The choice will be yours," says Bogdan.

"I am so grateful, and I have nothing left for me here in this city. I can tell that both of you love each other more than any humans I have seen. Perhaps I will have that someday and with whomever I please," replies Lillith who then finishes saying after a brief pause kneels down as a knight kneels before his king, "Absolutely my count and countess, it would be my honor to serve both of you."

Both Bogdan and Mariana smile at each other as they know they have made the right decision. Mariana says to Lillith, "Please, my child you don't have to grovel, we are not gods."

Bogdan adds, "Though some may think of us as devils," who waves his hand towards the cell door which opens instantly.

Without hesitation, Lillith follows Bogdan and Mariana as they exit the jail. For the first time in a long time, Lillith is optimistic about the future and feels like she is a part of a family once again.

CHAPTER 3

After leaving Milan with Count and Countess Vasile, Lillith would live and serve the Vasiles in their home in Medias.

She would learn their ways and their codes. At first, she would assist the Vasile's trusted ghoul Nicholas with daily chores. On her twentieth birthday, Lillith was initiated by Bogdan and Mariana and became a vampire.

It is the summer of 1646, much of Romania has been overwhelmed by leprosy. Where this has not physically affected the Vasiles and Lillith, it has disrupted their potential food supply. Also, many vampires across

Eastern Europe have been hunted down and killed by vampire slayers.

In the interest of maintaining a low profile and residing in an area where the blood supply is more available, the Vasiles relocate to Scotland, where they purchased a large castle much more significant and grander than their home in Medias, outside of the town of Kirkaldy.

The castle now named, Castle Vasile, lies on a small island in the North Sea which leads to the Atlantic Ocean and is connected to the Scottish mainland by a brick made bridge about a half a mile long.

Bogdan, Mariana, and Lillith are walking the down the hallway in the second story of the castle, where many of the bedrooms are. The walls are made of stone much like the exterior. Mariana exclaims, "as much as I miss our old home this castle is so much exquisite."

"Yes, my countess truly fitting for a king and queen," responds Bogdan.

"Hopefully, we will be safer from any slayers hear. Such an awful thing to have so many of our kind being purged like mere rodents," adds Mariana.

"Many of the other heads of the various vampire orders believe as I do, that something nefarious was behind these purges. Which is why we agreed to keep our initiations to a minimum as to keep a low profile by keeping our numbers low," replies Bogdan.

"Do you think I will ever be permitted to initiate?" asks Lillith with curiosity.

"In time and when it's safer and you are more experienced. Perhaps late next century," answers Mariana.

Lillith looks upon both Bogdan and Mariana with admiration as they have been her only true family. They have been saviors, mentors, and lovers to her, and she very much idolizes Mariana as a strong but passionate woman. At the same time, she also envies their relationship and hopes to have happiness as the Vasiles have. Maybe one day she will have her own order.

Lillith says, "My count and countess I have something I would like to announce."

"And what is that our dear, Lillith" asks Bogdan with curiosity.

"The both of you saved me and taught me a whole new world. I will forever be grateful and indebted to the both of you," Lilith says with slight hesitation and then announces as Bogdan and Mariana look on with anticipation and mystery," But I think after a few weeks it is time for me to move on and explore the world on my own."

Both Bogdan and Mariana are somewhat saddened to hear this news but at the same time proud that Lillith wants to be her own person and establish her individuality.

Mariana replies," I guess this shouldn't surprise us. You are such a unique and independent soul who needs to spread her wings. But we will miss you none the less." Mariana walks towards Lillith, embraces Lillith warmly and kisses her on the cheek.

"Yes, we will both miss you. As much passion and love as Mariana and I have for each other, we thoroughly enjoyed sharing that love and passion with you. You have been an obedient yet free spirited vampire. I fore see you will be one of the great vampires of our lineage," says Bogdan.

Lillith immediately embraces Bogdan, kisses him on the cheek, and responds," Both of you are the only family I have and that means the most to me. I will always visit."

"Our home will always be open to you. Where will you go first?" asks Mariana.

"I am not sure, I was thinking about Spain or France," replies Lillith.

Bogdan, who has the concerned look and feelings of a protective father says to Lillith," I want you to be careful. The purge may be over for now but mind your surroundings. As we have added Argyle as our newest ghoul, I will send Nicholas to accompany you as your personal ghoul."

Lillith is touched by Bogdan's generosity and replies, "I appreciate that so much my count, but I think I can take care of myself."

"We know you can but for our own sake please consider," says Mariana in a motherly tone.

"Very well besides it will be nice to have some company on my journey," replies Lillith with a smile.

*****

Lillith would travel across most of Europe over the following decades. Exploring and experiencing the customs of many cultures. She would feast on many depraved humans and become stronger as a result developing both physical and mental strength in such a brief time, that she almost rivals Bogdan and other more experienced vampires.

Besides satisfying her taste for blood she would take on many lovers satisfying her lust for flesh and desire. She would have no preference between men or women, preferring to have both at the same time but at last never finding her true soul mates which gradually makes her more cynical and quicker to judgement.

It is the autumn season in the late seventeenth century, Lillith is walking the streets of the Scottish capital of Edinburgh. After almost fifty years of touring Europe, she plans to return to Castle Vasile and visit her beloved Count and Countess Vasile as they plan on celebrating the festival of Samhain an ancient pagan holiday first practiced by the Celtics that the Vasiles have embraced since their relocation to Scotland.

It is extremely late this Saturday evening, almost midnight. It is hazy and cool with a slight fog appearing throughout the city. Though there are still sounds of gatherings amongst the people of the city. Many of whom drinking Scottish Ale and socializing with one another.

As she walks the streets, Lillith has hunger for blood and is searching for a victim to quench her thirst. A middle-aged lady wearing raggedy and grimy clothes with rips and stains present. Her hair is a mess yet despite her harsh appearance she gives off a delusional illusion that she is somehow the most beautiful woman of all of Scotland.

The woman who is a long practicing prostitute approaches Lillith and in a crude manor yell, "Hey there my lady. Are you lonely tonight? I can keep you company. I take with women as much as men."

The prostitute observes that Lillith may be a woman of wealth and the fact she is trolling the streets late at night in a shady section of the city makes her believe that Lillith is looking for some warm companionship if only for brief time.

Lillith looks back at the prostitute with disdain and in a dismissive tone says," Not this evening, I just feel an awful headache appearing just now."

"Oh bitch, are you are too good for us peasants is that it?," the prostitute says who is quite intoxicated on ale and without any shame also lifts up here dress exposing her bush to Lillith." This is the best in all of the city and its your fucking loss," the prostitute says as she slurs her words.

Lillith who is annoyed by the woman crassness and expresses a fraudulent smile as she walks with confidence towards the prostitute." I think you have changed my mind, and my headache has disappeared," Lillith says as she flips a gold coin towards the woman.

The prostitute has a gleeful and devious smile on her face and says," You won't be disappointed."

"I am sure I won't," Lillith says as she stares into the eyes of the prostitute who feels a strange sensation as she feels she no longer has control of her thoughts, words, or motions.

Lillith commands, "Get down on your knees, open your mouth, close your eyes, and stick out your vulgar tongue. I have something you can lick."

The prostitute does as she is commanded as Lillith wets her finger and caresses the tongue of the prostitute. The eyes of Lillith's turn blood red and fangs advance.

Lillith suddenly rips the prostitutes tongue and discards it. Before the prostitute who is in shock can even make a sound, Lillith thrust her right fist through the prostitute's mouth and out the back of her skull. With her left-hand Lillith grabs the prostitute by the throat slowly crushing it and ripping the prostitutes head right off.

Lillith pulls out her fist and begins slurping the blood off her hand. She tilts her head back as she lifts the decapitated head of the prostitute above her as she catches the dripping blood into her mouth which quenches the vampire's thirst for blood.

The thirsty vampire begins to devour the remaining blood from the corpse of the prostitute, as a young boy watches the horrid events from a dark alley by the home of the prostitute.

The young boy is disturbed by what he has witnessed and is frightened. But he sees the shiny gold coin Lillith had mockingly flipped towards the prostitute.

He begins to gradually crawl towards the gold coin hoping to go undetected by Lillith. He knows should she notice him that it would mean the end for him but as he is without money nor a home the alternative scenario would be to starve to death.

Lillith is down on her knees draining the blood from the dead prostitute and has her back to the crawling boy who reaches for the gold coin but as he does, a hand abruptly grabs him by the throat and lifts him in the air.

The hand of course belongs to Lillith. Once she notices the person, she has just grabbed is a child she gently lowers him back to the ground.

Lillith sees the young boy is petrified and turns her eyes back to hazel as her fangs disappear back into her mouth.

"Please don't eat me, I just need the coin to buy some food", says the young boy frantically.

"I am not going to eat you or drain your blood," replies Lillith in a calm and assuring voice," What is your name and how old are you?" she asks.

"My name is Ryan McAllen, and I am twelve," answers the raggedy boy who is nervous but a little at ease as it appears this woman is not going to kill him.

"Where are your parents? Where do you live?" questions Lillith.

"My parents are dead. Taken by illness. The rest of my remaining family left for the new world. My home is that alley over there," Ryan answers as he points towards the dark alley.

Ryan is a tall but skinny boy wearing a ragged cream color shirt and brown trousers. He has straight brown hair that almost covers the front of his dirty face.

He asks Lillith, "My lady, are you what they call a vampire?

"That I am, young sir. Why do you wish to be one?" asks Lillith.

Ryan responds, "Never really thought of it. But I really don't much care for sunlight and being a vampire couldn't be any worse than my life now. Are you going to turn me into one?"

"Not my power to do so," replies Lillith as a light drops of rain begin to fall. "And I am not exactly the parental type, but I don't intend to leave you out hear all alone," Lillith says as she hands the gold coin to Ryan.

"Let's find you something to eat and you can stay with me at the inn at which I am residing. My assistant, Nicholas, will see that you get cleaned up and maybe find you some clean clothes. If you like?" Lillith asks with a nourishing smile.

"Yes, sure thank you my lady but only if it is no trouble," replies Ryan.

"No trouble at all. "Now let's get out of this rain", responds Lillith. As Ryan follows Lillith she says," I am leaving for Kirkaldy tomorrow evening. I am visiting some dear friends of mine and I think they would be more than willing to give you a home."

"Are they vampires too and are you sure they won't mind?" asks Ryan with wonder as he follows Lillith.

Lillith turns her head and smiles at Ryan and answers," Yes, they are and many years ago they gave me a home and I wasn't much older than you are now. Since you have wonderful manners and I think they will take an immediate fondness to you."

Ryan responds with gratitude and eagerness, Thank you my lady. It would be an honor and I will be forever grateful to you and them, my lady."

"Thank you, Ryan, I can tell you are going to grow be a true gentleman and there is a massive shortage of those, and you can call me Lillith," with an assuring smile.

Lillith would introduce Ryan to the Vasiles. Like she presumed, Count and Countess Vasile allowed Ryan to stay with them without hesitation. Like Lillith before him Ryan would be raised and taken care of by Bogdan and Mariana.

Both Bogdan and Mariana enjoyed having Ryan at their home as it gave them a new family member they could mentor and teach the ways of the vampire and specifically the ways of their order.

On his twentieth birthday, Ryan would be initiated as a vampire in the Order of the Vasiles.

TALE 5: NEW YEARS EVE

CHAPTER 1

It is December 31, 2024, at Castle Vasile in Scotland. The Vasiles and their guests are finishing their dinner. A heavy clock gong is heard throughout the castle as the large grandfather clock erupts with a chime that echoes most of the castle.

The Vasiles, Ryan, Margaret, Lillith, and their guests are sitting in the enormous dining room, which has a high ceiling with three chandeliers that hover several feet over the extensive dining room table.

The aroma of roasted meat consumes the elegant dining room, which is lit with four candle sticks at each corner of the rectangular room and two candle sticks sitting opposite each other on the dining table.

Bogdan who is wearing a crimson red ruffled dress shirt and black pants with a black cape with red lining sits on one end of the table while Mariana dressed in revealing and sexy red and black corset leather dress, is sitting on the opposite end of the table adjacent from her devoted count.

Sitting on one side of the table to Mariana's left side is Margaret, Ryan, Lillith, Armand, and Elena. Sitting to her right is Winston, Akiko, Kevin, and Cheryl.

Finishing the last piece of bloody rare prime rib, Bogdan asks, "I hope everyone found dinner to be desirable."

Winston replies, "It was excellent, both the prime rib and the leg of lamb were perfect." Akiko adds, "Yes and the garlic mash was delicious."

"The mash is an old family recipe but our cook, Gertrude cooks it better than I," replies Margaret.

Mariana looks down the table towards Kevin and asks," So Mr. Price, Lillith tells me you manage horror conventions in North America?"

"That is correct Countess Vasile, they are called Scare-O-Cons and they have been quite successful," answers Kevin who briefly glances at Elena both of whom are nervous and mystified by each other's presence.

Cheryl asks Elena," Mrs. Gerhart, since you operate your own catering company that specializes in conventions, I assume you have met my husband."

Elena is caught off guard by the question and does her best to look calm and answers," Yes, our paths have crossed before. It is such a coincidence that we are all here tonight."

"I remember you telling me, honey about when you got the contract with Mr. Price's conventions," states Armand.

"Yes, that was a couple years ago, I believe," responds Elena who asks Kevin," Isn't that correct Mr. Price?"

I think it was about eighteen months ago if I remember correctly," answers Kevin.

Dread and angst both consume Elena and Kevin. They both think to themselves, 'Do our spouses know the truth about our affair? If so, why go through all this trouble bringing us to this bizarre dinner party? Surely this is not a coincidence?'

"I have to admit, I love a good horror movie, especially those demonic possession movies. "They are so absurd, they make me laugh," chuckles Bogdan.

"I like that one where that lady is up against the ceiling in the attic and starts banging the back of her head against the ceiling. Laughed my ass off, "says Ryan.

"I can't believe you laughed when that little girl stuck her head out the car window and got decapitated," remarked Margaret, "You have such a sick sense of humor my dear."

Ryan turns to Margaret as he deviously smiles back at Margaret while moving his hand up her inner thigh and says, "Ah she was a creepy little shit besides, that is why you love me, my dear, my sick sense of humor."

Margret playfully replies as she swats Ryan's hand away from her thigh like a fly and says," No my dear it's definitely something else."

The vampires at the table all laugh while the humans look befuddled that they would find humor in such a disturbing horror movie, and they are surprised by their crude humor except Winston and Akiko as they give a light chuckle as to play along with their boisterous hosts.

Lillith says seductively," I always loved those sixties and seventies British vampire films; so sexual and so bloody."

"Oh, I know they get me so wet", responds Mariana. "They sure do my love," Bogdan states with much pride."

"In Japan the horror genre has become quite popular especially extreme horror," adds Akiko.

"Yes, your country has produced some really brutal horror films," responds Margaret as Akiko nods her head in approval.

"I think we have embarrassed our guests long enough with talk of our sex lives. Let's adjourn to the ball room for more drinks and music before the ball drops to bring in the New Year. "We have hired some exceptionally talented entertainers," Bogdan announces as he and Mariana stand up.

Everyone else stands up at the table as Argyle, Gertrude and Victor enter the dining room to clean off the dishes and silverware from the table. The guests then follow their hosts out of the dining room.

Loud and up-tempo techno metal music can be heard from the ballroom down the hallway of the castle. Bogdan slowly opens the black double doors leading to the ballroom and says "Enter, my guests, the party has begun."

The six guests follow Bogdan and Mariana inside the ballroom while Ryan, Margaret and Lillith follow behind the guests. There are blacklights and strobe lights that energize the ballroom, which resembles more of a rave than a classic grand ballroom.

In the corner of the room is a fully stocked bar with two bartenders ready to serve the guests. A man and a woman with facial piercings and both having shaved heads are working the DJ stand.

In the opposite end of the room there is a large black curtain hiding the remainder of the ball room. The energetic room features gigantic floor to ceiling windows where the snow is seen falling from the sky.

Winston and Akiko are thrilled by the site and atmosphere in the ballroom as this is just their type of vibe. While Armand is somewhat amused as this brings him back to his youth. Kevin and Elena are bewildered and almost overwhelmed by the flashing strobe lights and the thunderous music, while Cheryl is somewhat annoyed and says to herself,' What is with these people. I'm not twenty-two anymore. I just want to get this night over with.'

Lillith announces, "Everyone make yourselves comfortable, get yourself a drink, relax or hit the dance floor. Whatever is your pleasure we will provide."

Bogdan and Mariana grab a bottle of old Italian wine and sit in their private booth by the bar where they can observe everyone.

After receiving their bar drinks, Lillith, the Gerharts and the Prices sit at a table not too far from the curtain.

Margaret, Ryan, Winston, and Akiko opt to not drink as they sit down at another table and begin sharing a marijuana pipe.

The black curtain rises and behind the curtain is a stage. Hovering above each end of the stage are cages where each cage features women dressed in black leather bras and shorts dancing provocatively to the music.

Appearing on stage a young vivacious lady wearing a red thong and two muscular men wearing only G-strings begin dancing and grinding up against one another.

A loud roar of applause and whistling comes from the table with Margaret, Ryan, Winston, and Akiko as they approve of the show. The four of them even go to the middle of the floor in front of the stage and begin dancing with one another.

At the other table Lillith is enjoying the atmosphere and the sultry bodies of all the performers. Secretly, Kevin and Elena, despite their inner tension, are actually amused by the show but are trying to contain their bliss.

Armand on the other hand is not hiding his enjoyment as he joins Lillith on the dance floor. Cheryl, however, is not amused and appalled by what she considers debauchery. Even when the woman on stage rips the G-strings off the two men unveiling all their glory, she doesn't even give them a second glance.

Elena is a bit bothered by her husband dancing provocatively with Lillith and excuses herself as she goes to find the ladies room. A few minutes later, Kevin tells his wife as he has to shout over the loud music, "I need to get my cigarettes from our room, I will be right back." "Fine, go," Cheryl says in a dismissive tone.

In the booth in the rear of the room, Bogdan lights a cigar and says," I wonder what those two are up to," referring to Elena and Kevin.

" Who knows?" answers Mariana with both curiosity and anticipation, "It will be fun to find out," as Mariana takes a puff from the cigar and both the count and countess look at each other and smile as they look up towards the cage dancers who are now topless and teasing about taking off their leather shorts.

The Addisons along with their hosts, Ryan, and Margaret, have returned to their table. Observing the female performer and her two male counterparts grinding their nude bodies up against one another, Winston asks," Are those three going to start fucking on stage?"

Ryan replies nonchalantly," Eventually they will get to it."

"Where did you find these performers?" asks Akiko with a joyful and astonished look.

"Amsterdam is where the Count and Countess found them. We have them over every New Year's Eve," responds Margaret.

Kevin is standing nervously in the hallway outside the ballroom near the restrooms. He is hoping Elena will re-appear soon as he knows they need to talk urgently about the bizarre circumstances they have found themselves in.

The hallway is dimly lit decorated with a few paintings of gothic art. As Kevin admires one particular painting depicting gargoyles, Elena emerges from the restroom.

Elena is both grateful and nervous to have the opportunity to finally be able to talk with Kevin alone. She says in an urgent tone, "Let's go over to this corner to talk where hopefully no one sees us."

The two secret lovers go to a dark corner down the hallway further from the ballroom entrance as Kevin asks Elena," Just what is going on here? This is so peculiar. They obviously know something."

"Armand says we were coming here to bring the passion back to our marriage. Which is why I had sent that text stating we should take a break from one another." Elena responds as she shakes her head in disbelief and states, "To think I almost believed him."

"Cheryl had told me a similar thing, but I was always a little apprehensive about it. She is not quite as effective as an actor as your husband apparently is," replies Kevin anxiously." If they do know. How did they find out and what do they have planned."

"Well Armand is a private investigator.," replies Elena who then has a moment of clarity as she has a look on her face as she has just figured out a complicated riddle and says to Kevin, "I bet this client that Armand was talking about from back in November was your wife."

With an agreeable look on his face, Kevin questions," That makes sense. But why bring us here? Why not just divorce us?

Answering in a panicked voice as she is worried something sinister is at play, Elena replies," I don't know but I fear it is not good. We need to figure a way to get out of here."

Kevin questions with a baffled expression, "But how? We are stuck in this castle miles away from the nearest town?"

Both Kevin and Elena look at each other with panic and anxiety as they ponder their escape. In the moment of the uncomfortable silence both feel an uneasy feeling of dread in their stomach as they both feel nauseous as if they might both vomit.

They both jump as they are startled by a voice right behind them. A gleeful female voice is heard," Hey there. We were wondering what happened to you two find folk," says Lillith.

Both Elena and Kevin, whose hearts are pounding, look towards Lillith wondering if she has heard their entire conversation.

Lillith reassures them that all is well by stating," You two shouldn't be so nervous. Your significant others love you both very much and realize the mistakes they have made. It is why they came to me for help."

Both Elena and Kevin are somewhat relieved but still puzzled. Kevin asks, "Why exactly would they come to you?"

Lillith comforts both Elena and Kevin and gently holds their hands and answers," Let just say, part of what we do here at Castle Vasile is help married couples either repair their broken marriages and or enhance them by taking their passion to an unprecedent level."

"And just how is that done, may I ask," asks Elena in a curious tone.

"You both will learn the answer soon. Armand and Cheryl have already been sent to a special room in the hidden part of this castle where they have a pleasant surprise for the both of you," answers Lillith who also says," Now it is eleven o clock now. I will deal with them as I am assisting them with their surprise. Why don't the both of you go back to the ballroom and enjoy the party and after the stroke of midnight I will return and escort you to your spouse's where all four of you will celebrate the New

Year in the most enthusiastic and pleasurable experience you have ever had."

Lillith then walks away from Kevin and Elena as they follow her and observe her walking up in a gliding manner up the spiral staircase. It is as if Lillith appears to be floating up the stairs,

Elena and Kevin look at one another in disbelief. Could Armand and Cheryl really forgive their actions? It does not seem to make sense but then again nothing about this night has made sense. Both Kevin and Elena feel some sense of relief but still wonder what this surprise could be as they return to the ballroom.

\

CHAPTER 2

It is late February of 2024 in Atlanta, Georgia, Kevin Price is sitting at a table in the hotel lounge sipping on his gin and tonic.

It is early Sunday evening and Kevin has just finished closing down his Scare-A- Con convention for the weekend and is relaxing.

Leisurely walking into the lounge is Elena Gerhart who had provided the catering for the convention. She notices Kevin sitting by himself watching the television in the lounge. Elena has known Kevin for about a year as she provides catering to all of his events, but their interactions are normally confined to business.

Feeling exhausted herself, Elena decides she could use some conversation and walks leisurely towards Kevin's table.

Looking upwards, Kevin notices Elena walking towards him. He has always found her to be attractive but as he is married and knows Elena is also married, has never bothered to talk to her in a more casual setting.

"Hello, Kevin is it ok if I join you? I hate drinking alone," says Elena.

"Sure, that would be great," Kevin replies who is blissful to have someone to commiserate with.

As Elena sits down at the table, a waitress instantly approaches the table and asks, "What can I get you?"

"A gin and tonic, please", answers Elena. "Make that two," adds Kevin.

The waitress replies," two gin and tonics coming right up."

"You are a gin and tonic man?" asks Elena. "Yes, it is my favorite," replies Kevin. "Mine too," adds Elena.

"The food was good as always, especially the fillets. Thank you once again for the service," says Kevin, who is just trying to make any type of conversation.

"You are welcome and thank you for the contract. These conventions of yours have been by far the most lucrative contracts, my company has," replies Elena who then glances at Kevin's wedding ring and asks, "How long have you been married?"

"Twenty-two years this June," answers Kevin as he stares grimly at his ring on his finger.

"You don't look old enough to be married that long," states Elena. "You must have gotten married quite young?"

"It was about a year after graduating high school. I had gotten Cheryll, that's my wife, pregnant so after our son, Shane was born we got married," responds Kevin, who stops to think as he smiles as he thinks of the good times his wife and he used to have and says, "To think both our children have grown up and are in college now."

"You must be immensely proud of them. Armand, that's my husband, and I decided not to have kids so we could both focus on our careers and us. Having children would have gotten in the way," replies Elena with a sigh. "Perhaps that was a mistake."

"Why, do you regret not having kids?" Kevin asks.

Elena answers," I used to think it was the best decision for us but now?" "But now, what?" asks Kevin.

"I don't want to dump my marital problems on you." replies Elena.

"It's ok," responds Kevin in an assuring manner. "It seems like you need someone to talk to. Besides, I don't have anything else better to do."

With a look of gratitude on her face Elena says, "Thank you. I actually do. All of my friends are his friends as well, so I don't know who to talk to. "

"We have been married almost eight years. We used to have so much passion and joy between us. It was like a fairy tale romance," Elena states with a smile as she reminisces to the time her and Armand first met. Her smile turns to a dower frown as she then adds" But in the last couple of years that flame between us as died down. Armand doesn't look at me in the same way as he used to. When I try to get him in the mood, he just brushes me off. I can't help to think if we had kids maybe things would be different."

    Empathy fills Kevin as he listens to Elena's story as his marriage isn't in the best condition either. Kevin replies, "Hard to say whether or not having kids would have made a difference or not. More than likely, it would have just delayed the inevitable."

    Kevin takes a long breath and says," You see things haven't been right between my wife and I for quite a while. Over the last several years. My wife has not only become cold and distant, but she has become an unpleasant person. She abuses me verbally, mocks me for what I do for a living, and sometimes belittles me both in private and in public."

    "If you don't mind me asking, how does your wife belittle you?," questions with curiosity as she herself at times has been criticized by Armand.

    "You have to understand, Cheryl was born into a wealthy family, who own the most successful real estate agency in St. Louis and is an only child. Her parents have always given her what she wants. You could say she was a bit spoiled, and I was brought up in a working-class family. My dad was an auto mechanic and my mother a teacher. I'm the oldest of three kids with two younger sisters. We had to scrape by and learned the value of a dollar," replies

Kevin." I say that for context. You see no matter how successful my Scare-a Cons are, my wife doesn't consider that a real career. She will tell people how embarrassed she is of what I do." Kevin pauses for a moment and continues," But what is even worse is she will complain how I don't satisfy her sexually."

"I am so sorry. No one deserves to be treated like that. You seem like such a nice person," responds Elena who is surprised by Kevin's response and begins to feel a connection like to wounded soldiers on the field of war.

"I know somewhat how you feel," assures Elena. "My husband says my ass has gotten too big and I should get a boob job. Now my boobs might not be the biggest, but I don't think they are that small, but I didn't think my butt was that big. But now Armand has me feeling like I am some kind of pig."

Kevin replies," I am sorry too for what you are going through. You don't deserve that either. You seem terrific too and if you don't mind me stating, I think you are exceptionally beautiful. Also, for the record your butt doesn't look too bad at all, not that I have staired or anything. And small boobs are just as nice as big ones, not to say that yours are small."

"Why thank you and I don't mind. I think you are quite handsome, Kevin," graciously replies Elena with a smile as it has been a long time since she has been complimented on her looks. "And for the record, I am sure you are more than adequate in the bedroom. Perhaps your wife should make an effort."

Both Kevin and Elena have a brief laugh then Elena's smile goes back to a frown and says, "I haven't felt particularly good about myself in a while. So, your words mean a lot."

"Because of the way your husband has been treating you? I know that feeling," asks Kevin.

"Yes, when you are being ignored and feel like being taken for granted it fucks with your self-esteem," answers Elena.

Kevin knows what Elena is going through and feels for her and then asks, "Would you like another drink?"

"Absolutely," replies Elena, "But let me buy this round." Elena then motions to the waitress to bring another round of drinks.

As the waitress brings the drinks Elena hands the waitress some cash and says," Please keep the change."

As the waitress leaves and both Kevin and Elena take sips from their drinks, Kevin asks," So do you ever think about divorce?"

Elena sighs and says, "Yes, of course, but part of me is still hoping our marriage can be repaired. What about you?"

"I have been thinking about it a lot. The kids are now grown but it would certainly be a messy and expensive divorce," replies Kevin.

"Well, if she is so unhappy with you. You would think she would want a divorce as well. You deserve to be treated better", says Elena as she thinks about her own failing marriage.

Kevin thinks how great his relationship with Cheryl used to be. He looks at Elena and admires not only her natural beauty even though she is just wearing a sweatshirt and some old jeans and not even wearing makeup but also feels a kindred connection with her. He says," And you deserve better to. It is nice to have someone to talk to about this. Especially, someone who is going through the same thing."

Elena appreciates the sentiment from Kevin. She feels an attraction to him as well. Although he might not be tall, dark, and handsome like Armand, he is still cute and seems to have a gracious personality which in her mind counts the most. She thinks to herself, 'If nether one of us were married, I would probably even invite him to my room. But then again it wouldn't surprise me if Armand was back home in Chicago banging some random slut. So why should he have all the fun.'

Looking into Kevin's blue eyes which matches the color of hers, Elena gives Kevin a flirtatious smile and says," Well maybe we both deserve better and maybe someday we both will have the guts to do something about it."

An hour later, Elena and Kevin are in Elena's room having sex. Elena is on top throttling Kevin's manhood and is yelling in ecstasy like she hasn't in a long time.

Kevin is grabbing on and clenching on Elena's ass for she is truly giving him a true thrill ride. At one point Elena whispers in Kevin's ear," You are more than formidable, and you definitely satisfied me". Which she doesn't just say to be nice. It is exactly what she feels.

Whispering back into Elena's ear, Kevin says with honesty," Your ass and tits are perfect for me."

Neither one even giving a second thought about their cold and unappreciative spouses. They are only focused on each other and a new passion that they have discovered with each other. They don't know where this will lead. Will this be simply a one-night stand between two scorned and damaged people? Or is this a start of a new romance that may be doomed to fail or may blossom like a rose seeing sunlight for the first time.

CHAPTER 3

Midnight has struck and the New Year of 2025 has been born. Celebratory sounds of kazoos and party poppers can be heard as everyone in the ballroom welcomes the New Year.

The female performer along with her two male counterparts are fornicating on the stage as the two cage dancers pleasure themselves.

Techno metal music continues to pound the walls of the ballroom like Roman drums. Winston gives his wife, Akiko, a passionate kiss after taking a drink of champaign straight from the bottle.

Margaret and Ryan both take turns drinking out another bottle of champagne before passionately kissing, twirling each other's tongues together.

Bogdan and Mariana observe the festivities with amusement as they gently and seductively caress each other.

Kevin and Elena watch in bewilderment. They wonder whether or not to succumb to their own desires or wait a few minutes for Lillith to arrive. They think to themselves perhaps their fidelity is being assessed and therefore will not give in to temptation.

Lillith enters the ballroom with a devious gleam on her face. She takes a handkerchief and wipes fresh blood off her mouth as she walks towards Kevin and Elena.

"Come with me. It is time that the two of you become reunited with your lovers," Lillith says to Kevin and Elena, who stand up and follow Lillith out of the ballroom.

As the three exit the room, several sprinklers attached to the ceiling begin spraying the room and those in it, but it is not water, it is spraying fresh human blood.

The two cages with the dancers lower to the stage as they exit their respective cages. Fangs now appear from each of the dancers as they embrace in erotic passion.

The three performers on stage; the two men and the woman also grow fangs as they are joined by the two dancers as they all take turns licking blood off each other's sultry bodies.

Covered in blood from head-to-toe Margaret digs her teeth into Akiko's neck as Ryan does the same to Winston.

Mariana, who has removed Bogdan's pants and lifts up the skirt of her dress is riding her count's passion rocket with her wet love canal.

Bogdan who is still sitting back up against the black leather booth he and his countess were sitting in pulls out and exposes Mariana's boobs one at a time and slowly licks blood off of the large mounds of pleasure which only excels Mariana's passion as she feels her clit getting hotter and wetter.

Like many previous New Year's celebrations, The Vasiles have once again started the New Year with a trues orgasmic bang.

*****

On the third the top floor of the castle, which is four stories tall, Lillith leads Elena and Kevin down a dreary hallway. The hallway is almost dark if not for a few lighted torches mounted to the wall.

Unlike much of the rest of the castle which is draped and decorated in an elegant yet gothic themes combining the old with the new, the fourth floor mirrors the hidden dungeon that resides below the castle dark and gloomy with lifeless features. It is as if the past spirits of days haunt this floor long gone.

Lillith, who is holding a torch, leads Elena and Kevin who follow closely behind. Kevin is in awe as he feels like he is in the setting of a horror movie. It is what enticed him to make this journey in the first place when his wife, Cheryl, suggested to spend the New Year's here at Castle Vasile.

An anxious sensation consumes Elena as she closely follows Lillith. She is uncertain about what awaits her and Kevin. She hope it is some type of surprise that their respective spouses have planned. Elena is trying to remain optimistic, but she is getting the sense that something is not quite right.

"So where exactly are we going?" Elena inquires.

"To a special room," answers Lillith who stops in front of a double door at the end of the hallway." A room I specifically use to help couples regain their magic long lost but needs to be found," adds Lillith.

The creaking of the doors are heard as Lillith opens them. It sounds like the hinges haven't been lubricated in decades.

As the doors open, Elena and Kevin peer into the shadowy room which actually looks comfortable and welcoming. There are two red velvet couches on opposite ends of the room that is noticed. As they enter the room and several paintings depicting vampires, werewolves, goblins, and other grotesque creatures of the night.

Amazed and captivated by the paintings, Kevin thinks to himself how these would make great exhibits at his conventions and wonders whether the Vasile's would consider selling them.

Elena is, also, finds the paintings remarkable as she has grown an infinity for gothic art due to her time providing catering for Kevin's conventions.

Lillith walks towards the doors as if she is leaving the room but stops and turns towards Elena and Kevin and says," I will take my leave now. Your loving spouses will join you soon and happy New Years."

Lillith exits the room and closes the double doors behind her.

Both Elena and Kevin observe a glass door that leads outside opening. A frigid wind begins to blow inside the room as snow follows the breeze. They both feel the chill from the breeze.

They assume the harsh wind blew the door open but before they could close it, Cheryl emerges from the outside terrace. She is wearing a white sleeping gown and has a radiant and seductive look about her, a sharp contrast from her refined and conservative attire, she was wearing earlier.

Kevin who is bewildered by the look of his wife has a confused look on his face and asks," Honey? Is that you?"

"Of course, my dearest love. I hope my appearance pleases and arouses you.?" replies Cheryl in a seductive tone.

Kevin is both bewildered, yet pleased as he has not seen this side of his wife in several years.

Elena looking around for Armand asks, "Where is my husband?"

Elena is then startled as she feels the touch of a hand on her shoulder and hears the calm words, "I am right hear my dear," responds Armand as he appears out of the dark behind Elena as if he materialized out of thin air.

Surprised and stunned by her husband, Elena asks, "Armand, what is all of this?"

"Cheryl and I, who was my client both realized how awful we have been to you both," answers Armand.

"Yes, we know of your affair, but it was us who drove the both of you to each other. But Armand and I decided we would do something special to repair the damage," adds Cheryl.

"So, you know of our affair, and you are not angry?" inquires Kevin who would think for sure at the least is wife would be full of rage.

"We were at first, my husband," answers Cheryl in a calming and assuring tone.

Armand adds," But we sought at Lillith who made sus look at the situation from a different perspective."

"We realize we are just as much to blame if not more to blame for your actions," says Cheryl as she turns towards Kevin as her hazel eyes gaze at his blue eyes.

Armand then turns towards Elena and says in a loving tone, "Tonight we will make it up to you both. We will have a night of passion and ecstasy and we all owe it to our wonderful host Lillith."

Old romantic feelings begin to consume Elena. She stares at her husband and notices his shirt is unbuttoned halfway down, partially revealing his muscular chest.

Elena embraces her husband and gives him a passionate open mouth kiss, which Armand returns.

After the kiss, Elena says, "I love you and I am so sorry." Armand replies, "I love you too, but I am the one who should be sorry. Now let's have a seat and enjoy the show our new dear friends have in store for us."

Both Armand and Elena have a seat on the couch and observe Cheryl as she gently sits Kevin down on the adjacent couch across the room from Armand and Elena. Cheryl disrobes exposing her nude body to everyone. She climbs on top of Kevin and begins to kiss and gently nibble on his neck while Kevin fondles Cheryl's breasts. It has been a long time since the couple have engaged in anything remotely this enthusiastic.

Watching this unfold, Elena is aroused with inner ecstasy and turns towards her husband and asks enthusiastically," I have to ask. Where is this leading" as she wonders if she is about to participate in an orgy which secretly she has always wanted to do.

Armand turn towards her and responds, "Something so fantastic that you can't even imagine."

Cheryl slowly unbuttons Kevin's shirt and begins kissing on his chest working her way deliberately down to his crouch. On her knees she unzips his pants and pulls out Kevin's rock-hard dick.

Kevin feels such a feeling of relief and pleasure fills his whole body as his has been given new life.

Cheryl begins lightly nibbling on Kevin's ever filling testicles, her hazel eyes suddenly turn a shade of blood red, and fangs begin to form. With one violent motion she rips Kevins balls out of his sack. Kevin yells and cries out in excruciating pain as Cheryl sadistically laughs.

"Oh my god, what the fuck!," Elena screams and stands in horror, but Armand grabs her from behind and throws her back to the couch.

Elena in terror notices that Armand's eyes have turned red and now has fangs growing out of his teeth as drool is seeping from his mouth.

"No, no what the hell are you?" screams Elena. Armand laughs and replies with rage," I am an instrument of revenge you stupid treacherous bitch. Did you really think I was going to forgive you and that loser you fucked."

Armand rips Elena's dress and says, "You like it rough. I seem to remember you loved it when I would bite on your tits and nipples."

Using his teeth, the newly initiated vampire, Armand rips his wife's left nipple off then takes a massive chunk off her left breast and begins sucking the blood from her.

It is ironic as the part of the female anatomy used to give life and nourishment to a newborn is now giving life and power to a vampire with the difference being that Elena will methodically have her own life drained from her.

Screams and cries of torturous anguish from Elena and Kevin fill the room but as the room is soundproof, no one outside can hear their screams.

With blood dripping from her mouth, Cheryl holds Kevin's testicles in front of him to see and says tauntingly,

"Looks like I have taken your manhood now I will drain your life from you."

Crying but trying to be brave, Kevin responds defiantly," You took my manhood a long time ago you fucking crazy cunt, but Elena gave it back to me."

With rage in her face, Cheryl, now a vampire, has the strength twice as strong as Kevin and smacks his jaw with the back of her hand. She jumps on top of him and yells," You and her cunt, girlfriend will endure the worst painful death anyone can possibly imagine!" as she rips into Kevin's throat sucking his blood.

As Armand mutilates Elena's breasts with his sharpened fangs like a wolf feeding on a dead deer, she stares over towards Kevin with tears running down her cheek. She feels responsible for both her and Kevin's impending demise as it was her who approached him in the hotel lounge that fateful February night in Atlanta. She cries not for herself or the physical pain she is feeling but what her dear friend, Kevin is going through. Consumed with guilt she thinks to herself, 'He doesn't deserve this. It is my own fault. If I could sacrifice myself to save him, I would but it is too late.'

Kevin, who is slowly having both his blood and life sucked out of him, begins to age. His hair, skin and even his eyes begins to turn a dirty grey. He looks over at Elena and also feels remorse towards her but despite her grotesque appearance as she too is turning grey, he also feels love and affection for her. She restored a passion within him and will always be grateful to her. Kevin hopes that there is an afterlife as he accepts that both Elena's and his time in this life and this world is coming to a tragic end.

To himself he grieves as his old love who once symbolically sucked the life out of him is now literally sucking the what remains out of him as Cheryl moves over and bites into the other side of his neck. But he has hope that perhaps if there is another life after this that he will be reunited with his new love, Elena. Kevin begins to feel sorrow as he realizes he will miss seeing his children graduate, get married and have kids of their own. The doomed man begins to recite the Lord's prayer to himself and accepts his fate.

Armand has now thrusted his fangs into Elena's throat as Elena looks over towards Kevin. Her whole life flashes before her eyes. She sees herself as a little girl cooking her first batch of cookies with the help of her parents. She thinks how heartbroken they will be. Will she receive a proper burial, or will her parents wonder with dread what happened to their daughter. What lies will Armand tell them? Elena remembers her school days and her childhood friends. She reminisces about graduating culinary school in Chicago, how she wished she had gone to Paris instead. But she smiles as she reflects on the day she signed the paperwork creating her catering service, her proudest achievement.

Lillith re-enters the room with a conceited and proud look on her face as she witnesses Elena and Kevin who now look to be a hundred years old take their last gasp of breath and leave this world.

"I think their dead now my new friends", says Lillith with a smile.

Both Armand and Cheryl back away from the dead corpses of their former spouses and smile at Lillith as Armand ask," What now our Countess?"

"As we discussed before. The both of you will hide in your coffins down in the dungeon. Then as the Vasile's and the others lay in theirs, shortly after we will destroy them in their sleep," replies Lillith with a sour look on her once joyful face which has turned to a spiteful look.

Lillith walks towards the glass door and looks outside as the snow falls. She turns around and says to Armand and Cheryl whom she has recently initiated," I will then rule this castle and you will serve as my lieutenants. Now throw their bodies off this balcony into the rocks and ocean waves. It is best we leave no traces of them."

Armand and Cheryl do as they are commanded and drop the rotted corpses of their departed spouses off the balcony like bags of trash.

In the corner of the room unbeknown to the vampires inside a mouse is seen as it may have witnessed the tragic events.

The mouse scurries through a crack in the baseboard of a wall in the room and runs through the small passage within the walls of the castle.

The frantic mouse finds its way back into the hallway and has a metamorphosis as it transforms into the shape of a young woman. That woman being Margaret McGregor.

She leans up against the wall, heartbroken to learn the news of Lillith's impending betrayal of Bogdan and

Mariana. She knows what she must do and transforms into a bat flying down the four stories of Castle Vasile.

TALE 6: THE VAMPIRE AND THE SERPENT

CHAPTER 1

It is the turn of the twentieth century in New Orleans, Louisiana on an early overcast spring morning as the sun is trying to break through the grey gloomy clouds which promises rain will drop. The air is thick with humidity as steam can be seen rising from the ground.

Two young boys are seen playing in the streets of the downtown area of New Orleans. They are throwing a baseball around when one of the boys overthrows his friend and the ball lands in an alley.

Both the boys run eagerly towards the alley. As they search for the ball, they can smell the stench, something like a dead animal. But instead of a dead animal they stumble upon a body of an elderly looking man. At first glance the young boys believe him to be hobo passed out from a night of drinking liquor.

One of the boys shrieks in shock as he backs up, points at the man, and says," Look at his neck." The other boy sees an enormous chunk of the man's neck missing as it has been ripped apart. The boys run from the alley and begin to yell for help.

The commotion catches the attention of a man and woman who happen to be having a morning stroll. The man stops the children and asks, "What is the matter?

One of the boys answers as he points towards the alley, "There is a dead body in there."

"You two stay here." The man says and looks to his wife "Sally, stay here with these two children, while I take a look."

"Ok, but be careful, Robert," the woman says to her husband.

At this moment, a deputy arrives as he too heard the hysterical yelling from the boys. "What is going on here?" demands the deputy.

"These two boys say they have discovered a dead body in this alley, and I was going to check on him as I am a doctor," answers Robert.

"You are a doctor? From here in New Orleans?" the deputy asks.

"Yes and no. my name is Doctor Robert Reynolds, and this is my wife, Sally and we are only visiting for the week. "We are from a small town in Texas," Robert answers as he extends his hand to the deputy.

"My name is Deputy Stephen Marlowe. Please to make your acquaintance but let's check on this poor soul," replies Marlowe.

Marlowe and Doctor Reynolds enter the alley and discover the man laying on a pile of garbage.

As he squats down next to the body, the doctor doesn't know what odor is worse; the stink from the garbage or the foul stench from the man, who the doctor examines and notices a piece of the man's neck missing.

Looking down at the doctor and the male corpse with curiosity, Marlowe asks, "Is he dead, doctor?"

"I am afraid so. Look at this nasty gash on the side of his neck," responds the doctor.

"I don't see any blood. With a wound that severe, there should be blood all over the place," observes the deputy.

"There should be, but it is like something sucked the blood right out of him. Look how grey he is," says the doctor.

"The blood sucked out of him. Like a vampire? Don't tell me you believe in such nonsense," asks the deputy.

The doctor stands up and looks at the deputy and thinks for a moment as he remembers a tragedy from his childhood, when an evil demon known as the Hangman murdered his father, and replies," In my experience, anything is possible.

CHAPTER 2

Later that evening as mist fills the air and one can smell the moisture. A youthful and radiant brown haired Italian woman is seen walking the streets of the French Quarter of New Orleans. She is a sophisticated lady and despite not having a husband appears to be a woman of means as she is dressed in an elegant royal blue dress accentuating her voluptuous curvy figure that is made from the finest tailors in France.

The young woman is Lillith Tesio, a loyal vampire of the Vasile Order and initiated by Bogdan and Mariana Vasile.

Lillith is now one hundred and eighty-seven years old but like all vampires has retained her youthful glow as she has not aged since her twentieth birthday. As long as vampires feed on the blood of the living, they will retain their youth and Lillith is no exception.

Lillith admires the autumn damp weather as it is her favorite type of weather as she surveys the French Quarter. She notices a mixture of horse-drawn wagons and auto mobiles which are sometimes referred to horseless carriages.

She stops to admire one of the automobiles and marvels at this new piece of machinery and thinks how such an invention could come to be.

The smell of beer swill and boiled crawfish fills the air as Lillith walks past several restaurants and drinking establishments.

Lillith ponders if she will come across any deviants in this city as she did with a man the previous evening who thought he was going to rape her. The same man whose body was discovered earlier that morning. Like her mentors Bogdan and Mariana, Lillith chooses only to feed on humans who are of immoral and unethical character.

Lillith longs to find the type of love and passion that her count and countess have. Lillith admires the Vasiles as they saved her from mortal doom but envies their King and Queen relationship and the power and influence, they possess among the vampires. As she sees herself as a princess, she is ever seeking a prince or perhaps a princess or both as she has no preference between the two genders.

She sees a large two-story home, and she stops and takes a precise look at the house as she admires the architecture of the building. It is painted white with six large pillars connecting the bottom floor with the top floor from the exterior. The upstairs has a massive outdoor terrace that equals the size of the front porch area on the first floor.

Bulky oak trees are seen standing in attention like Soldiers guarding Buckingham palace on the left side and right side of the house. A black iron fence that stands five-foot-tall surrounds the perimeter of the property.

The house is owned by Gabriel Montague, a Frenchman of wealthy means who immigrated to the United States a few years ago. He is mainly known as a satirical writer but also an occultist known for his blasphemous writings and his suspected practice of black magic. In fact, he is known to many as the Serpent, equating him with the Anti-Christ.

Some say the Serpent conducts human and animal sacrifices, worships Satan and enjoys torture. At times

Gabriel enjoys and pretends to live up to those tales of gossip but in all reality most of those rumors are untrue, though he has committed animal sacrifice and certainly practices magic.

He is an aspiring wizard who believes that all people have the potential to transform into higher beings even gods as they pass from this life to the next, just to various degrees of power and believes in the power of the individual spirit and that all people can achieve an elevated spiritual plane through magic and sexuality.

He lives by a slogan, "The Will is the Law" a phrase he coined in his book, *The Book of Thelema*. Thelema being a religious philosophy Gabriel created and has spread all through Europe, Northern Africa and now North America.

He sees himself as a prophet who communes with the supernatural entity, Aiwass, whom Gabriel says provides the basis of the beliefs of the League of Thelema. Gabriel, who believes it is his destiny to transform into an omnipotent god in the next life, wishes to spread this philosophy all over the world and replace the other old religions as the dominant faith.

Lillith has read Montague's works and has sought out both him and his League of Thelema as she is seeking more self- fulfillment. She enjoys the life of a vampire but wants more and believes that combining the laws and practices of the League with being a vampire will help transcend her into something special and powerful. Hopefully will lead to her discovering her true mate, who will be her count.

As she stands in front of the gate which creeks as she opens it, Lillith feels raindrops slowly and lightly pelting her skin as rain begins to lightly shower the city.

Entering the property Lillith follows the stone path that leads to the front entrance of Montague's house. She walks up three steps made of brick and is now standing on the porch in front of the double door entrance made of wood.

Before Lillith can knock, the doors opens and standing in the doorway is a young and thin Brazilian woman named Angelique, who smiles and greets Lillith, "You must be Lillith the vampire. The master said you would be arriving tonight."

Lillith is stunned that Angelique knows of her identity as a vampire and asks," You know that I am a vampire?"

"Of course, my darling," Angelique replies in a reassuring voice, "Don't worry we are accepting of everyone. Our order holds vampires along with witches, pagans and werewolves in high regard and we are honored to have you with us."

This sentiment brings great comfort to Lillith as this may be the first time since becoming a vampire that she has been welcomed by non-vampires, who know of her identity.

Lillith asks," I understand Master Montague received my letter."

"He did, indeed and has been eagerly awaiting your presence. "Now follow me down this hallway," answers Angelique.

Lillith follows Angelique, who is wearing a black robe, down the hallway, which has a wooden floor with the walls of the house painted white. At first glance the elegant homestead appears to be a normal New Orleans home.

Angelique, with Lillith walking beside her, enter a large room at the end of the hallway. The room is almost empty other than several dressers with shelves that occupy the room There are eight other people in the room, four women and four men are present. Some are dressed in similar black robes to Angelique, some are removing their normal clothes, and some are naked as they prepare to dress themselves in the robes. Lillith is impressed with the diversity of the group as they all appear to be from different walks of life.

Angelique announces, "Attention everyone, we have a visitor for tonight's ceremony. This is Lillith."

Everyone enthusiastically welcomes Lillith who greets them back.

A black robe is handed to Lillith by Angelique who says," You will need to remove your clothing and jewelry and place them in this dresser. Don't worry, it will be safe here. The ceremony starts at Midnight. In about fifteen minutes from now I will lead everyone to the upstairs where Gabriel will be waiting for us."

Moments later Lillith and the eight other followers follow Angelique up the stairs to the top floor. Unlike the bottom floor, which was luminously lit, the upstairs is dark with a few candles providing light in the hallway.

They pass one door on their left. Then the next door, which is on everyone's right hand side is entered by the enchanting group.

The room is dark with a few candles lit to provide some light. The candles give off an intoxicating aroma as they smell of mahogany. The floor is made of hardwood but has a red rug in the middle of the room, At the end of the room there is a wide altar with a black cloth covering it and two candles on each end of the altar, neither of which are lit.

Angelique walks towards the altar as Lillith and the eight others kneel down on both knees on the rug.

A voice is heard from behind the altar," Welcome my friends to our monthly Midnight Ceremony of Thelema." At the end of those words the two candles at the altar and four candles in two-foot-tall holders at each corner of the rug light up on their own in a mysterious fashion. Lillith is surprised to see them light up by what appears to be magic. Though the rest of the followers have seen this before and are not surprised.

Behind the altar Gabriel Montague is now seen. He is, also, wearing a black robe but his has gold trim across his shoulders. He is of average height with short brown hair and devilish brown eyes. He has a slight French accent but speaks English along with four other languages so fluently that most people barely hear his accent.

He addresses the followers," Tonight, my friends we have a special and unique guest. Among us we have a representative of the undead. We have our new friend, the vampire, Lillith. whom I know you have already met."

Gabriel emerges from behind the altar. And walks towards Lillith who is in the front row to the side. Gabriel motions to Lillith to stand up and Lillith stands as she looks Gabriel in the face and their eyes meet as Gabriel says, "Welcome Lillith I am pleased to have a vampire with us especially one from such a prestigious order."

Lillith impressed by Gabriel's knowledge responds, "You know of the Vasiles?"

"I know of them but have never had the pleasure of meeting them", answers Gabriel.

"It is a pleasure meeting you Master Montague and an honor being among the League of Thelema", Lillith politely replies as she bows and kneels back down with respect."

For the next hour, Gabriel praises Aiwass and reads from the *Book of Thelema.* Gabriel had sacrificed a goat before the ceremony and passes a chalice of the goat blood around for everyone to drink from. He emphasized to Lillith that where she and other vampires drink blood for physical nourishment that the followers of the League of Thelema drink blood for spiritual nourishment.

Lillith takes part in the blood drinking and over the course of the night becomes infatuated with Gabriel. She is in awe of his intellect and his charm. Despite his average looks, Gabriel more than makes up for it with his wit and charisma.

Gabriel addresses the followers," The will is the law and discover your own truth and act on it." The master of the league looks around the room at the followers and pronounces as he lifts his arms in the air like a magician attempting to levitate an object," Now to conclude tonight's ceremony as we always do. We will now engage in Eroto-Comatose Lucidity. Everyone disrobe and find your partner."

As the followers including Lillith remove their robes, Angelique asks," Master, we have an odd number of participants tonight?"

"Yes, Angelique you may join Harold and Michelle. I'm sure they will not object."

Lillith observes everyone and is surprised to see that not only that two of the women partnering with each other but also two of the men as well, as she suspects that this Eroto-Comatose Lucidity, whatever it is, may be some kind of sexual ritual. Only in the vampire orders is this type of homosexual behavior respected and considered acceptable.

Gabriel who is also disrobed approaches Lillith and says," You can pare with me if you like."

"I would be honored but what exactly is eroto-comatose lucidity, it sounds sexual," asks Lillith.

"It is a ritual that is part sexual and part spiritual. It is way to unleash and ease tension and conflict by achieving an orgasm through meditation with some physical stimulation but no penetration," answers Gabriel.

Lillith who finds this ritual enticing replies, "That does sound stimulating except the part of no penetration." As Lillith tries to attempt to sound disappointed.

"It might not quite be as satisfying as actual fucking, but you will receive spiritual enlightenment," Gabriel responds as he gazes into Lillith's hazel eyes and also says to her, "Follow me. We will perform this ritual in my primary bedroom."

Lillith takes Gabriel's hand, and they leave the sanctuary and walk down to the far end of the hallway and enter Gabriel's bedroom.

The bedroom is enormous with a door that leads to the front outdoor terrace. A large black rug is positioned on the floor in front of the massive king-sized bed which has four posts at each corner of the bed.

Gabriel sits down in the center of the rug and crosses his legs and asks Lillith, "Sit down and cross your legs around me.

Lillith does as Gabriel requests and wraps her arms around his neck as Gabriel holds onto Lillith's butt with both hands.

"Now we will stare into each other's eyes for a few minutes until I say to close them", says Gabriel.

After seductively gazing into each other's hypnotic eyes for a few minutes Gabriel says," Now we will shut our eyes. I want you to think about everything that troubles you and then think how much better you can make your life. Try to discover what it is you desire and how you can achieve that."

Lillith takes a deep breath and closes her eyes. She thinks how she still feels inferior to Bogdan and Mariana and how secretly lonely she is. Sure, she could seduce any person she wants but like Bogdan yearned for an equal which he found with Mariana; Lillith desires the same thing.

Captivated with Gabriel, Lillith feels an intimacy with him as she can feel her heart beating faster. 'Is this love that I am feeling, surely not. I have just met this man, this mortal. Would he allow me to initiate him?', Lillith asks herself.

Lillith begins to feel an inner calmness and serenity. Her mind is clear as to what and whom she wants. She begins to feel a moistness in her vagina as she can feel Gabriel's shaft getting harder as it is gently rubbing on the outer walls of her clit.

Panting in pleasure, Lillith gradually feels an unexpected ecstasy as Gabriel has not even entered her as he said he wouldn't. She can hear Gabriel breathing heavier and senses his arousal and can imagine Gabriel fucking her hard and fast.

Lillith moans as her pussy is drenched. But she feels her fangs beginning to form but now is not the time. She is able to control her vampire impulses and the fangs shrink back into her jaw and without warning she feels an intense orgasm and she can feel and hear all the other followers joining in the same sensation. She moans in delight.

Gabriel looks at Lillith and asks, "So how did you enjoy the ritual."

Almost speechless and astonished, Lillith is able to catch her breath and says," Unbelievable, amazing, and yet insightful. I learned a lot about myself."

Lillith looks down and notices Gabriel is till erect and says," Did you not orgasm?"

"Internally yes but I have trained myself to control when I cum. I wanted to save that for later," Gabriel says with a charming smirk.

Instantly and without hesitation, Gabriel and Lillith begin to kiss passionately. Lillith whispers in Gabriel's ear, "I want you. I want you to fuck me."

Gabriel answers back, "Why do you think I brought you to my room?"

The both stand up and Lilith asks, "Have you ever fucked a vampire before?"

"No, but I am looking forward to it" answers Gabriel. "Have you ever heard of sadomasochism?" asks the wizard in a sharp and dark tone.

"I have. It is essentially pain and torture mixed with the pleasures of sex. Am I correct?" responds Lillith who is thinking what devious and suggestive plans Gabriel has in store for her.

"That is the simplified version of it I suppose" replies Gabriel who then says," You see I believe the path to true pleasure is from pain. I can tell you very much desire the ultimate pleasure."

"Yes, I have had many pleasurable experiences with both men and women, but I have never had a connection with anyone like I just had with you while were in engaged in Eroto-Comatose Lucidity," replies Lillith.

"I felt a strong connection with you as well. Will you allow me to introduce you to the exhilarating thrills of sadomasochism."

Lillith who is typically the aggressor and prefers to be the dominant one in a sexual relationship but has always wanted to be submissive to a man if she thinks he is deserving, drops to her knees and looks up to Gabriel and says, "You can do whatever you want, just give me the ultimate pleasure, my master."

"Very well, rise to your feet", commands Gabriel in an assertive tone. As Lillith rises, Gabriel walks around her slowly like a shark circling its prey. He is surveying every inch of her nude body and is impressed with her beauty but thinks what pain he can inflict. Gabriel grabs a blindfold out of a mysterious black satchel and covers Lillith's eyes then has her open her mouth as he gags her with a black piece of cloth.

Lillith is anticipating what Gabriel will do to her as the mystery and suspense thrills her. But she is somewhat fearful, 'What if Gabriel is secretly a vampire slayer who means to murder me? Surely not, after all it was I who sought him out not the other way around.'

Gabriel orders Lillith to raise her hands above her head and restrains her hands together with a pair of old iron shackles and connects the shackles to the top brace connecting two of the bed posts.

Lillith is now stretched out vertically. She is now helpless and in a state of submission. Gabriel reaches into the bag and reveals two metal clamps that resemble clothes pins and snaps them on each of Lillith's nipples. The pain at first is sharp and unexpected for Lillith who shrieks a bit feeling the arduous pain.

"Don't worry my beauty, I will probably take it easy on you for your first time", says Gabriel cryptically as he raises a handheld wooden paddle and swats Lillith's bare butt several times.

At first the abrasive strikes hurt her ass but after the first few swats, she begins to like it and barely acknowledges the pain of the nipple clamps.

She is excited even more when Gabriel drops the paddle and begins spanking her with his bare hand. Lillith can feel herself getting wetter with each strike and begins to feel like she might orgasm as her sounds of pain turn to echoes of ecstasy.

Gabriel himself is in a euphoric state as the experience of inflicting pain onto Lillith gives him a sadistic pleasure. So much so that the arousal of Lillith's muffled screams helps him maintain his erection.

The sexual sadist grabs Lillith from behind and forcefully places his forearm across and up against her throat like a wrestler placing his foe into a headlock. Though he loosens the grip a bit to allow Lillith to breath.

Gabriel fondles Lillith's breast with one free hand while he mercilessly removes the metal clamps from her rosy nipples. As he squeezes her breasts, causing her to become stimulated. Kissing and nibbling at her neck and shoulder, Gabriel's wandering hand slips down toward Lillith's velvety netherlips and begins rubbing his fingers over her clitoris. Lillith felt like she was going to scream, but with the gag in her mouth, all that came out was muffled moans.

Releasing Lillith from his clutch and removing her gag and blindfold, Gabriel looks into Lillith's eyes as Lillith pleads, "Don't stop."

Gabriel smiles devilishly as he leaves Lillith shackled, he drops to his knees and lifts her legs over his broad shoulders and begins planting his tongue into Lillith's pussy, exploring every region.

The intensity of her near orgasm returns, and this time Lillith is able to scream at the top of her lungs. Gabriel even begins to gently bite on her clit which makes the feeling even more intense as Lillith orgasms intensely.

She is released from her shackles by Gabriel and without hesitation grabs him by his throat and forcibly pushes him onto the mattress of the bed.

Lillith in a cruel but playful voice says," Now it's your turn. Let see how you like pain, my dear."

"You will have to do better than that, bitch," responds Gabriel in a defiant tone.

Lillith violently turns Gabriel on his stomach and begins to smack his ass with the paddle which keeps Gabriel excited as he is someone who loves to endure pain as much as he inflicts pain.

Lillith also begins spanking Gabriel with her hand but then digs her sharp nails into the bottom of his neck and deliberately scratches all the way down his back and onto his butt. The scratching causes some bleeding on Gabriel's back and though Lillith is able to hold back her fangs she cannot refrain from her blood lust urges and begins to lick the blood off of Gabriel's back who is amazed and thrilled by her behavior.

At last, the sexy and alluring vampire, who has now taken charge turns the peculiar wizard on his back. The seductive vampire grabs a lit candle nearby. She slowly and teasingly rubs her pussy across Gabriel's throbbing cock.

As Gabriel feels the sensation, he eagerly awaits to be inside Lillith who suddenly mounts his rod with her twat grabbing his manhood.

As Lillith begins riding Gabriel, she slowly pours some of the melted wax from the candle on Gabriel's chest, who yells in anguish but instead of the pain of the hot wax causing him to shrink inside Lillith instead he feels his shaft getting harder.

Lillith can feel Gabriel's love muscle pulsating inside her and as she orgasms again, Gabriel takes the candle from her and rubs the hot wax onto Lillith's breasts which both burn in torment but also in ecstasy.

Hopping off his cock kissing Gabriel; lips to lips and tongue to tongue. She slowly makes the journey down Gabriel's toned chest to his stomach before reaching the great treasure of his anatomy and begins seductively licking the tip of his skin rocket in a teasing fashion before sucking on Gabriel's man meat back and forth in a steady motion.

Gabriel can feel his testicles filling up with semen. His penis erupts inside Lillith's mouth like a volcano erupting lava. As Lillith disengages gurgling and swallowing his seed, the domineering dark wizard becomes the aggressor once again and throws Lillith on her stomach as he is still hard.

Pulling Lillith's hair back like a rider pulling the rains of a horse, he hears Lillith begging for him to enter her once again. Gabriel obliges and thrusts several times inside her drenched sex sponge. Both enjoy the violent and forceful penetration. Gabriel thrusts faster and harder inside Lillith who has never been fucked this extreme before. She screams with erotic pleasure and both the lovers orgasm together.

This fateful night unexpectedly impacts Lillith in more ways than she could have imagined. Besides the powerful and intense sexual event, she experienced with Gabriel. She, also, experienced a spiritual awakening and has more confidence in herself than ever before.

Lillith wishes to serve Gabriel's every need as she hopes he will serve her needs. Faithfully believing he will be her loyal mate and one day will submit to initiation and both could become two of the more infamous vampires ever.

CHAPTER 3

Just a few months pass by after that night of destiny since Lillith first encountered The League of Thelema and their charismatic leader, Gabriel.

Lillith spends quite a bit of her time with the one many people reveal as the Serpent, learning everything she can about his teachings and self-fulfillment as she discovers her love for the expert wizard.

The vampire believes the time has come to profess her love to him and ask if he would join her in initiation to the world of vampires and be her count.

It is a hot and humid late summer evening in New Orleans. A sultry scent can be smelled throughout the city. After having an intimate dinner Lillith and Gabriel are now relaxing in his study in his house. The room is filled with bookcases along every wall of the room. The cases consumed with many books ranging in subjects from philosophy, ancient religions, history, and occult practices.

The study smells of incense and candles. Gabriel looking outside the floor to ceiling window outside the back of the house is dressed in black pants and a white satin ruffled shirt.

Dressed in a scantly black dress with red trim that accentuates her thin and busty features, Lillith with some hesitation as her nerves hit her stomach and her heart begins to pound faster, slowly walks towards Gabriel who has his back turned to her.

"Gabriel, my cerebral teacher and animated lover, may I have a word with you?" Lillith asks nervously.

Intrigued by the tone of her soft-spoken words, Gabriel turns around and gazes at Lillith's eyes and replies," Cerebral and animated? I like those adjectives. I can tell something has been on your mind all night, and now you have gained the courage to ask me."

Taking a deep breath, Lillith who has never been this nervous at least not since she was jailed and set to be sent for inquisition before being rescued by the Vasile's says," What I have to say is important."

Pouring himself a glass of absinthe and gives Lillith and encouraging looks as he takes a drink and responds," Say what you have to say my lovely vampire."

Finding both the courage and words Lillith pronounces," Gabriel, I have had the grandest and the most fulfilling time over these last few months and I have come to realize." Lillith pauses for a few seconds and stairs straight into Gabriel's eyes and states with assertion," I love you and wish to spend the rest of our lives together."

Suspecting that Lillith's feelings for him were becoming stronger and more enthusiastic, Gabriel is not as surprised to hear these delicate words from Lillith's mouth. Gabriel replies, "I see. You almost sound like you are proposing marriage."

"Of course not, marriage is a nothing but a ceremony of ownership as you have put it," reassures Lillith.

Impressed with Lillith, Gabriel says," Very well, you have listened and learned from my teachings. But my radiant black rose, whereas I care for you very much. I cannot say with certainty that I love you. Love is a foreign concept to me, and I am not the type to be committed to one person."

Feeling she may have come on too strong, Lillith quickly corrects herself," Oh, of course I understand that. Even though the Count and Countess are bonded together like a King and Queen both have had many lovers even sharing them."

"And you wish to have with me what they have?" asks Gabriel.

Lillith answers with confidence as she has gained her courage," Yes, I do and why not? I am a vampire of one of the most prestigious and influential Vampire orders and you are wizard, a master of the magical arts and the most intelligent being I know. Together, we can spread Thelema across the globe and dominate society as you have dreamed, my love."

Lillith pauses and walks up to Gabriel putting her arms around him and asserts," I can even initiate you as a vampire and with your knowledge and abilities you would not only be the most powerful vampire even more powerful than Bogdan or Mariana but the most powerful being in this world and I will be there beside you."

Gabriel is astonished by Lillith's passion and her ambition. Qualities he has admired in her since they first met. He acts as if he is considering her offer and says with certainty," I have much admiration for you and your kind but immortality in this world is not my goal. My destiny, my dear, is to pass from this world into a greater world, there I will achieve true immortality. I will be a god."

The wizard also known as the serpent backs away from Lillith and arrogantly announces," Furthermore, vampires are sterile, and I mean to spread my seed as much as possible so when I leave this world, my bloodline will continue my work and promote all that I have taught."

Feeling desperate Lillith pleads," Very well my master, my love you remain a mortal until your time has come but until then allow me to serve and stand by your side as your loyal queen. I cannot have children, but I will pledge to watch over them. I can teach and guide them. You can show me how."

Sternly, Gabriel looks at his vampire lover and asks," So this is your will?"

"The will is the law", recites Lillith which is Gabriel's primary commandment.

"Unfortunately, it is not my will and you have become too attached. You can still serve the League of Thelema but not here. If you are as loyal as you state, I will send you to Russia to spread my message there," responds Gabriel with a cold and heartless pitch.

Feeling scorned and now angry, Lillith responds," Send me away, like some peasant? How dare you? You are just like everyone else, always dismissing me. Always taking me for granted."

Lillith's eyes begin to turn red, and her fangs emerge, and she screams defiantly, "Well no more! I now will take control of my life because it is my will!"

Most people in Gabriel's position might be afraid and trembling with fear at the sight of a disturbed vampires with drool pouring off her fangs but instead remains calm as he motions his hand towards Lillith and says a few ancient words and before Lillith can strike at Gabriel, she freezes.

Lillith is confused and shocked by her lack of movement but now scared as Gabriel has demonstrated he has the power to annihilate her if he wishes.

"How dare you raise your voice to me in my house," scolds Gabriel without raising his voice and asks, "Is this how you treat your teachers and your betters. I am sorry my dear, I enjoyed almost every minute of our time but now I will banish you from here and cast a spell where you will not get anywhere near this house nor me."

Lillith begins to feel a change inside and outside of her as Gabriel raises his hand and points at Lillith who begins to transform into a bat but not by her doing by Gabbriel's magic.

Another window opens through Gabriel's will and with one swift motion of his right hand, Lillith's bat form is flung through the open window upwards towards the night sky before plummeting several miles away from Gabriel's house.

Landing in a disgusting and vile alley way. The serpent has vanquished the vampire. Lillith, now having control of herself, transforms back to her human form. Whimpering in sadness and humiliation, Lillith rises to her feet and yells at the top of her lungs.

The outraged vampire then spots a young boy that is most likely an orphan who is trembling in fear of the vampire in front of him.

Lilith regains her composure and says with a reassuring smile to the child," Come towards me. I have something for you".

The child feels compelled to do as Lillith commands as she has learned the power of hypnosis. Not any older than ten years old, the boy walks towards Lillith.

With an ominous smirk, Lillith says "Children, the future of humanity". With one violent motion Lillith uses her right hand and clutches the child by the throat crushing his larynx.

In a blood thirsty and rage filled frenzy, Lillith feeds on the boy's blood sucking him dry.

For that moment, Lillith has discarded all that she was taught from the Vasile's about their rules and their code. Going forward Lillith will live by her own rules and feed on whoever she pleases. One day when the time is right, she will take her place as the ruler of Castle Vasile.

TALE 7: THE MASTER AND THE STUDENT

CHAPTER 1

Just a few hours after the annihilation of Elena and Kevin, Lillith stands alone in the courtyard that is located at the rear of Castle Vasile.

It is cold outside with the smell of salt water in the air from the ocean. The light snowfall has stopped on this early New Year's Day morning, though the ground is covered with a standard layer of powder like snow. It is still pitch dark outside and the moon is barely present as most of it is obscured by the ominous clouds.

The sizable courtyard can be entered through a back entry way of the castle and is surrounded by a towering brick wall. During the spring and summer, the grounds would feature forest green grass which is now slightly covered by the snow. The courtyard would also contain many thriving plants and blooming flowers that now lay dormant during the winter.

A modest size fountain lies in the middle of the courtyard but the surface of the water in the fountain is covered by a layer of ice.

Despite the above freezing temperatures. Lillith stands patiently in the courtyard gazing upwards towards the partial moon wearing only her black strapless corset dress as vampires have a keen tolerance to the sometimes-harsh elements of the weather especially temperatures whether they be cold and frigid or hot and balmy. A few hours from now the sun will soon rise and the other vampires in the castle will soon retire to their coffins.

Lillith had dispatched her newly initiated vampires, Armand, and Cheryl, to their coffins in a separate wing of the castle away from the others as other coffins maintain the dungeon that lies beneath the castle. The cunning and vindictive vampire has plotted her shock attack on the other vampires as she relishes the thought of taking control of the castle.

A gleeful smile appears on her milky white face as she fantasizes about establishing her new vampire order. 'Castle Tesio has such a formidable sound to it,' Lillith ponders to herself.

The double glass doors to the courtyard swing open. Lillith's treacherous smile turns to a frown of concern as Bogdan and Marian enter the courtyard with Ryan and Margaret following obediently behind them.

Lillith is startled to see her fellow vampires. She had figured they would all still be engaged in wild and untamed sexual exploits to celebrate the new year. Lillith thinks to herself that maybe they are planning to invite her to partake in another orgy in which case that would be a convenient way to keep them all distracted.

"Happy New Years's, Lillith. We had wondered where you had run off too. Tending to your new vampires?" cordially and casually asks Mariana.

"Of course, I decided to leave them to their own devices. I believe Armand and Cheryl will make find additions to the order", answers Lillith who is of the impression that the Vasiles suspect nothing of her treasonous agenda."

Ryan asks, "And what of the other two you brought here. What were their names again?"

"I believe their names were Elena and Kevin", responds Margaret. "They seem like such nice people."

"Well, they weren't," asserts Lillith who feels that the other vampires in her presence suspect nothing of her devious plans." They were truly awful. The way they abused their spouses is unconscionable. Both the new recruits fed on them and disposed of their remains."

Becoming annoyed with this whole conversation as Bogdan knows exactly what Lillith has been up to, as the others are aware as well but are playing coy. The count on the other hand who is outraged is done playing games and sternly says, "Enough of this bullshit Lillith, we know what you are up to. You are planning to kill all of us with your new lackeys."

The feeling of her stomach being punched stuns Lillith as she thinks how they could know. Lillith maintains her innocence and defends herself. "My count how could you say such a thing. I have always been loyal and obedient towards you and Mariana."

"Quit the lies, Lillith, I witnessed and heard everything", says Margaret with a grim look on her face. "You along with your new vampires set up Elena and Kevin and I heard all your plans to take over."

Lillith on the defense is outraged by the accusations and pleads as she turns to Mariana and Bogdan, "Are you really going to believe this insolate little twat?"

"How dare you throw stones at Margaret. She has no reason to lie," responds Mariana who is both heartbroken by Lillith's betrayal and irate. "My count and I rescued you and made you one of us. You have been like family ever since."

Knowing she has been caught, Lillith now owns up to her dastardly deeds, and defiantly pronounces" Fine you are right I was going to kill you. And why not you both have had your turn now it's mine to rule. It is my destiny and my will and always has been."

Angry and disappointed, Bogdan asks, "What happened to you? Perhaps we coddled you too much. Because your words and actions are that of a spoiled brat."

"Spare me the lecture Bogdan," boldly replies Lillith," Your many initiations were nothing more than producing pawns of you and your whore wife. You just wanted an army of obedient vampires to serve your every need and bloat your egos. You are just as selfish, and power driven as I am but at least I admit it."

Mariana, who has loved Lillith like a daughter, then a sister is filling with rage but is trying to contain her emotions and keep her wits about her which is a quality learned from Bogdan, says to Lillith," How long have you felt this way? How long have you been plotting?"

Bogdan also asks," And where is our ghouls? I haven't seen any trace of them since after midnight."

"I have been plotting this for quite some time. Well over a hundred years", replies Lillith who then picks up a brown burlap bag that was sitting in the now near where she is standing. "As far as your ghouls go. I terminated their employment."

Opening up the bag with a malicious smile, Lillith turns it over and the severed heads of Argyle, Gertrude and Victor fall to the ground with three lifeless thuds.

In shock and confused by Lillith's actions and cryptic words, Ryan who has remained noticeably quite during this vocal altercation as he has adored Lillith like an older sister, finally breaks his silence with outrage in his voice," What have you done and why? They did nothing to you and all we did is show you love. I suppose your ghoul, Nicholas, met the same fate and did not perish in an accidental fire as you claim?"

"Oh, poor Ryan, always such an optimist and a willing pawn. They all had their opportunity to join me but like a bunch of mindless buffoons chose death instead" replies Lillith in a condescending tone and then appeals to Ryan's confusion and boyish nature," I remember rescuing you from poverty and delivering you to the Vasiles. Perhaps I should have kept you to myself and raised you. It is not too late though. You could join me and be my count."

Being once enamored with Lillith even as an adolescent when he first met her, Ryan clears his thoughts as he is much cleverer than Lillith realizes and responds," Nice try but you can't manipulate me like you did Cheryl and Armand."

Disgusted and surprised by Ryan's response, Lillith replies with disdain, "How pathetic", then turns to Bogdan and Mariana," So now what. It would seem we are at an impasse."

"Normally, I would kill you where you stand but I'm willing to give you a chance. We will banish you instead. Never to return to this castle or Scotland for that matter," Bogdan retorts in a scolding and scornful voice.

Feeling no fear and all too confident in herself, Lillith responds boldly, "I don't think so, Bogdan. I won't make it that easy. You will just have to try and kill me. The question is who is going to try first. I will kill each of you one at a time?"

Feeling responsible for bringing Lillith into the Vasile order in the first place all those centuries ago, Mariana answers with no hesitation, "I will," as Mariana takes off her cape and kicks off her high heels wearing nothing but a black leather corset with crimson red trim.

This is just what Lillith expected, she suspected Mariana would want to confront her, teacher versus student. "Very well you old bitch. You have gone complacent and soft over the decades, and you will be no match," Lillith says mockingly.

"You still don't know shit, Lillith. Never mistake my happiness for weakness," Mariana responds boldly as salivating penetrating fangs emerge from her mouth. Mariana's fingernails have transformed into piercing sharp claws as her eyes turn red as blood.

Lillith instantaneously reciprocates Mariana's transformation with her own. Now both have fully converted into their complete vampire forms.

The two vampires move closer and begin gradually trying to circle one another. Anticipating unwearyingly for the first strike. But who will strike first as both Mariana and Lillith begin to snarl and hiss at one another.

Instantaneously the two vampires leap towards each other grabbing each other's throats midair before collapsing to the ground where Mariana lands on top of Lillith still grasping at Lillith's throat who still has her hands locked on Mariana's throat.

The two vampires roll over each other on the damp snowy ground with each trading off positions from being on top in control to being on bottom on the defense.

Mariana assumes control by positioning herself on top of Lillith attempting to pin her down by the throat as the two new adversaries continue to grasp each other's gullets and faintly scraping their claws in each other's necks.

Lillith is able to extend her arms bench-pressing Mariana above her and vaults her rival off of her as the two disengage from each other.

The countess lands on her feet trying to regain her breath and turns around towards her younger opponent who has flipped from the ground back on her feet.

Feeling the damp chill air in their lungs as they observe their breath in the air as they exhale but the frigid elements have trivial effect on them.

Charging with intent, Lillith swipes at Mariana's face with her claws slightly scraping the countess's cheek as she was able to avoid the full force of the swipe. However, Mariana was not able to avoid a thrust from Lillith's clenched fist at Mariana's chest knocking the countess backwards.

Not giving her adversary time to recuperate, Lillith delivers a karate style front kick to Mariana's face, plummeting the countess to the ground.

Both Margaret and Ryan are concerned and appear as if they wish to intervene on Mariana's behalf but Bogdan who senses their uneasiness with the situation motions to them to back off and says deliberately and with assurance," Don't fret, my countess can handle Lillith. After all she was trained by the best."

Lillith is wickedly grinning as she is confident that she has the advantage over Mariana, the woman, the vampire, and countess she once held in such high regard. The sweet taste of victory feels so close to Lillith.

However, Mariana regains her composure and stands back up defiantly as she wipes some blood off her nose and face. She returns a devious smile back to Lillith and says, "Is that really the best you have my young student?"

Lillith with brashness states, "On this day the student will defeat the master and the rest of you one by one." Lillith then aggressively charges at Mariana growling and goes to strike her former master in the face but Mariana who senses Lillith has now let her pride get in the way of her better judgement blocks the incoming punch and thrusts a blow of her own towards Lillith's rib cage knocking the breath out of Lillith. Without hesitation, Mariana's delivers a striking round house kick to her former student's face who collapses to the ground.

On the warpath, Mariana picks up Lillith from the ground by her throat and lifts Lillith's body up in the air by one hand and slashes Lillith's exposed stomach with her free hand as Mariana's claws rips through Lillith's belly.

Dropping her enemy to the ground she observes the exposed internal organs of Lillith who is now gasping for air and coughing up charcoal black blood. The severely wounded vampire is holding what used to be her belly as she is desperately trying to keep her intestines and stomach from falling out of her.

Before Lillith can mutter a word, Mariana grabs Lillith by her hair tilts her head back and rips the younger vampire's esophagus out with her piercing fangs in which the older more experience vampire spits the bloody organ onto the snowy ground next to Lillith who is now on her knees and defenseless.

Lillith is unable to make a sound gasping for air while being consumed with her own blood that looks like tar. She wonders how Mariana was able to get the best of her so easily. It is as if Mariana was only toying with her the whole time. Bogdan once taught Mariana to let you adversary come to you first to observe their tactics and techniques, then counter those tactics and use them against the adversary.

Knowing this fight is nearing its conclusion, Bogdan reaches inside his black trench coat and unveils an old Romanian broad sword. The same sword he used when he vanquished Micheal the Brave all those centuries ago during the Fifteen Year War. The count walks towards his bride and tosses the sword to her as she catches it with one hand while holding fer fallen enemy's head up with the other.

The younger vampires: Ryan and Margaret look upon Mariana with amazement as they have only known her as cultured and proper motherly figure unaware of her warrior nature and fighting tendencies which has always been a part of her personality even before her fateful meeting with Bogdan who merely unlocked Mariana's true self.

The Countess of the Vasile holds the sword firmly in her hand and looks down on her impending victim and remembers back on the night the her and Bogdan first met Lillith and how they rescued her from that jail cell. She reminisces about raising Lillith as if she were her own daughter and how proud of her, she was.

A tear is seen running from Mariana's eye and down her cheek. She looks up towards Bogdan who has been her husband, her rock, and her salvation. Bogdan notices the look on Mariana's face. A look that says that she cannot go through with it. As angry and hurt as Mariana is at Lillith's betrayal, she cannot bring herself to bring the final blow of death to her former friend and now enemy.

The countess tosses the sword back to her count but still holds Lillith head up right by the top of her blood-soaked hair.

Receiving the sword, Bogdan walks gradually toward Lillith. He himself is saddened by these developments as he also loved Lillith as a daughter. Why couldn't she just accept banishment instead of engaging in a fight she was only doomed to lose?

Attempting to contain her grief and her tears, Mariana with sadness in her eyes says to Lillith," I do not know what we did or didn't do to lead you to this moment, but this could have been avoided."

Bogdan clutching the sword in his right hand and holds it up against Lillith's neck and says in a cold and hurtful voice, "Damn you for forcing us into this position." With those words the count pulls the sword away from Lillith and with one swift stroke from the piercing weapon separates Lillith's head from her body which collapses to the frigid ground.

Mariana tosses Lillith's decapitated head next to the lifeless and headless corpse. In much despair Mariana turns immediately from everyone and walks briskly towards a corner of the courtyard.

Bogdan looks over towards Margaret and Ryan and directs in an authoritative voice, "Take her remains and burn them. Spread her ashes into the sea."

"What of her two new vampires; Armand and Cheryl?" Ryan asks.

"They may very well have been maneuvered by Lillith, but they made their choices, and it would appear that two innocent souls lost their lives because of their choices,' answers Bogdan who pauses with some regret but states with certainty," Dispose of them however you wish. Just make sure it is done before the sun rises."

"What of our initiated vampires, Winston, and Akiko? Should we have them assist us?" asks Margaret.

"This is the time of their rebirth and a time for all of us to celebrate their addition to our order. Let them rest. We will tell them the tales of these tragic events," responds Bogdan. "Now go. You haven't much time."

Ryan and Margaret gather the remains of the fallen vampire, Lillith. Bogdan walks towards Mariana who is still standing in the corner of the courtyard and staring upward towards the sky and takes a deep breath as both her and her husband can smell the scent of salt water which is carried by the breeze from the sea that surrounds Castle Vasile.

Bogdan places his hand on Mariana's shoulder as the countess states, "We should have seen her betrayal coming. We could have avoided all this ugliness."

"I know my love", replies Bogdan. "Perhaps Lillith was right. Perhaps we have grown complacent."

Mariana turns to face her count and gazes into his eyes. Bogdan gazes back at her. They both have a look of sorrow and regret for what has just transpired but still have a look of love and faithfulness towards each other. Count and Countess Vasile embrace the passion, trust, and admiration they have for one another for over the past five hundred years that has never waned.

CHAPTER 2

Later that morning, a few minutes until the sun rises, Armand awakens to the thunderous sounds of ocean waves slamming into the shoreline and is startled and perplexed to discover that he has not awoken in his coffin but instead is outdoors tied to a post outside the grounds of Castle Vasile overlooking the Firth of the Forth sea. Behind him, tied to the same post facing the opposite direction is Cheryl who is still asleep.

"Cheryl, Cheryl, wake up," Armand frantically pleads.

Opening her eyes and seeing the castle from the outside in one direction and the ocean from the other as the aroma of salt water permeates her senses, Cheryl who is both confused and delirious questions, "What the hell is going on? Why aren't we in our coffins?"

"How the fuck would I know?," answers back Armand who is agitated." This isn't good whatever has happened."

"It is that treacherous bitch, Lillith. She probably sold us out to save herself. I told you we shouldn't have trusted her", Cheryl responds in a pretentious tone.

"You never said anything. I swear all you do is bitch. No wonder Kevin cheated on you," responds Armand who has become annoyed with Cheryl.

"Fuck you.", Cheryl harshly counters." You were cheated on as well. So, you are not exactly husband of the year either."

"Will you two knock it off," says a male voice with a heavy Scottish accent. It is Ryan who, along with Margaret, appear from the back gate of the castle.

Margaret adds, "Yes really. Why Lillith ever thought you both would make good vampires is beyond me."

"Lillith sold us out, didn't she? ", questions Cheryll. "What lies she has told you. It is not true. She coerced us. I swear."

"She didn't betray you. You betrayed yourselves and showed poor judgement in defiling Castle Vasile in the way you did," Margaret says in a scolding attitude.

Accepting that they have been caught, Armand asks, "So what is to become of us?"

"Oh, in about ten minutes from now, you will find out," Ryan answers with a boyish grin.

"In the meantime, my dear friend and I need to get some beauty sleep. It has been a long night, and we are exhausted" Margaret adds as she has a girlish smirk on her face.

Holding and swinging their hands together like two teenagers who have a crush on each other, Ryan and Margaret begin walking hastily back to the castle singing the old Scottish folk song, *Auld Lang Syne*.

As Ryan and Margaret make their way back to Castle Vasile, Cheryl screams in fear, "Please don't leave us here. We will do anything you ask!!!" But her pleas for mercy are ignored as Ryan and Margaret vanish inside the confines of Castle Vasile.

Armand knows what is about to happen and accepts his fate. Perhaps he deserves this punishment but smiles knowing he vanquished Elena first.

Cheryl feels cheated and believes she deserves better than this but has always felt shortchanged her entire life as well as feeling entitled to the best that life has to offer.

Creeping up from the horizon the sun rises and begins to cast light where there was darkness. An ocean breeze brings a frosty chill to their bones. As there are newly initiated vampires both Armand and Cheryl are still sensitive to the harsh elements of the weather unlike more mature vampires.

The chill of the ocean breeze gives away to a burning sensation within their blood which feels like boiling water as the sun continues to rise. Both Armand and Cheryl, now in arduous pain, catch a glimpse of the radiant light emanating from the sun.

Both are trying to keep their eyes shut to avoid looking at the sun but begin to sweat from the internal and external heat they are feeling. A moist fiery steam emanates from their scorching bodily surfaces and they both begin to scream in anguish and torment.

The steam transforms to a light smoke and the stench of burnt hair and skin originates from both Armand and Cheryl. They are still attempting to keep their eyes closed but the interior of their eyelids begin to burn.

Having no other choice they both open their eyes hoping for relief but instead their eyeballs burst into flames and their hair on their bodies singed. Their skins begins to sizzle and melt like candle wax and their high pitch screams can be heard from a long distance.

The burning sensation that originates from the sun causes their smoldering bodies to burst into flames as their remains explode with a roar and their remnants are nothing but a powdery grey dust that spreads and disintegrates into the wind.

The road to vengeance that Armand and Cheryl ventured on inevitably lead to their gloomy destruction as did Lillith's lust for power, who allowed her broken heart at the hands of Gabriel Montague to define her destiny instead of using that cruel experience as a motivation to perceiver.

Winston and Akiko Addison who are now initiated as vampires of the Vasile Order would return to Japan seeking potential recruits for the order returning at least once a year to pay homage and respects to the Count and Countess by presenting new recruits and remaining loyal to the order.

After the tragic destruction of Lillith, Bogdan and Mariana, whose hearts were broken from the painful incident, would decide in time, that they would begin to groom Ryan and Margaret as eventual successors as the eventual count and countess of the Vasile Order and rulers of Castle Vasile, which for almost four hundred years as served as the home and epicenter of all vampires belonging to the prestigious Vasile Order.